The Drowned Heiress

Calvin Hill

Published by Calvin Hill, 2024.

This is a work of fiction. Similarities to real people, places, or events are entirely coincidental.

THE DROWNED HEIRESS

First edition. October 23, 2024.

Copyright © 2024 Calvin Hill.

ISBN: 979-8227773449

Written by Calvin Hill.

The Drowned Heiress
A wealthy heiress is found dead in her family's private lake, and the detective must sift through the family's dark history to uncover the truth.

The lake was always still. Its glassy surface had reflected centuries of secrets, holding tight to the dark whispers of the family who owned the sprawling estate perched on its shores. But that morning, the stillness was broken.

Charlotte Winthrop, the last of the Winthrop heiresses, was found floating face down in the family's private lake. Her white nightgown rippled in the water, a ghostly silhouette against the murky depths below. To the outside world, she had everything—a vast fortune, a lineage of prestige, and the promise of a dazzling future. But beneath the glamour of the Winthrop name, dark currents swirled.

When Detective Jonathan Marlowe arrives at the scene, he is met with a family cloaked in grief—and suspicion. The Winthrops, pillars of society, are no strangers to scandal, yet none could have anticipated this tragedy. The drowning seems accidental, but something about the scene feels wrong. Marlowe knows there is more to Charlotte's death than meets the eye.

As he begins to unravel the twisted threads of the Winthrop family history, Marlowe is drawn into a world of old money, bitter rivalries, and buried secrets. Everyone in the family has something to hide, and the more he digs, the clearer it becomes: someone wanted Charlotte Winthrop dead. But who? And why?

In a tale where the weight of inheritance can drown as surely as water, Marlowe must wade through decades of lies and deception, uncovering truths that threaten to destroy the Winthrop legacy—and possibly take him down with it.

Some secrets, after all, were meant to stay submerged.

Chapter 1: The Founding

The lake was still, perfectly undisturbed in the pale light of dawn, as though time itself had held its breath in deference to the sprawling Winthrop estate. Its glassy surface reflected the towering mansion in the distance, a symbol of wealth and status that had dominated the landscape for generations. The grandeur of the house seemed to mock the silence of the morning, its towering windows dark and cold as the sun crept over the hills.

It was the lake that everyone talked about, the one at the center of it all. The one that had swallowed Charlotte Winthrop whole.

No one could quite recall when the lake had first been dug out, but it had been there since the earliest generations of Winthrops took root on this land, a private retreat for the family and an emblem of their enduring wealth. The lake wasn't large—more of a mirror-like pool that sprawled behind the estate—but it was deep. That was the rumour. Its depth had been a subject of local fascination for years. No one knew exactly how far it went down, only that it was cold, murky, and uninviting. And now, it had claimed one of their own.

The morning began like any other, quiet except for the distant hum of estate workers tending to the grounds. It was the gardener, an old man named Samuel, who first saw the pale, drifting shape in the water. He had been trimming the hedges along the shore when he looked up, his weathered hands freezing mid-snip. From the distance, it seemed almost like a white flower floating, caught in the soft breeze that barely stirred the water. But as he squinted through the early morning mist, he saw the unmistakable outline of a body—delicate, motionless, drifting just beneath the surface.

"Dear God," Samuel muttered, dropping the shears and running towards the lake.

By the time he reached the shore, his breath coming in ragged gasps, the reality of what lay before him was undeniable. The body was facedown, the white fabric of Charlotte's nightgown swirling around her like a shroud. Her dark hair spread out in tendrils across the water, framing her lifeless form in an almost grotesque beauty. Samuel's heart pounded as he staggered back, his hands shaking as he fumbled for the small radio clipped to his belt. He pressed the button, his voice barely a whisper.

"Call the house. It's Miss Charlotte," he said, the words catching in his throat. "She's dead."

Within minutes, the entire estate was awake.

Charlotte Winthrop's body had been carefully pulled from the lake by the estate workers, laid gently on the grassy bank as they waited for the authorities. Her skin was cold, the pale blue of her lips a stark contrast to the vibrant green of the surrounding gardens. A soft breeze whispered through the trees, but the air felt heavy, suffocating with the weight of something unspeakable.

The house staff huddled together at a distance, their whispers mingling with the wind. They spoke of her in hushed tones—Miss Charlotte, the golden child, the heiress to the Winthrop empire. She had been the face of the family, a symbol of the old wealth that had defined the Winthrops for generations. Her father, William Winthrop, was a titan of industry, his wealth extending far beyond the rolling hills and manicured gardens of the estate. And her mother, Eleanor, was a woman of stature and refinement, known for hosting lavish parties that brought together the elite of society.

But Charlotte had been different. Beautiful, yes. Privileged, without question. Yet there had always been something distant about her, something that set her apart from the rest of the family. She had not been the socialite her mother had once hoped for, nor had she been content to settle into the role of dutiful heiress. Instead, Charlotte had spent much of her life withdrawing into herself, a figure of both fascination and mystery within the walls of the mansion.

Rumours had swirled around her for years—whispers of a secret lover, of falling outs with her family, of a restlessness that no amount of money could soothe. But none of it had seemed to touch her. She moved through life as though she were untouchable, her aloofness only adding to her allure. Until now.

As the sun rose higher in the sky, casting long shadows across the estate, a low murmur spread through the gathered staff. Someone had to call the police. The realization struck with the force of inevitability. The housekeeper, an older woman with greying hair and a stern expression, took the lead. She disappeared into the house, the heavy doors closing behind her with a resounding thud.

Inside the mansion, the news spread even more quickly than it had among the staff.

Eleanor Winthrop sat frozen in her private parlour, her hands trembling as she clutched a porcelain teacup. The air was thick with the scent of jasmine, but she could hardly breathe. She had barely said a word since the housekeeper had informed her, her face pale as her mind raced to comprehend the impossible. Charlotte, her only daughter, was dead.

William Winthrop, on the other hand, was a man of action. He stood near the window of his office, staring out at the lake with a hardened expression, his jaw clenched as if refusing to show any sign of weakness. He had always prided himself on his strength, his ability to navigate the cutthroat world of business with an iron will and an unflinching determination. But this—this was beyond his control.

It had been hours since Charlotte was found, but no one had yet called the authorities. The family lawyer had been summoned first, as if there were some way to contain the scandal before it spread beyond the estate gates. But deep down, William knew the truth. The news of Charlotte's death would be the crack in the foundation of the Winthrop empire. And once the world learned of it, there would be no stopping the flood.

Finally, after what seemed like an eternity, the housekeeper returned to the Parlor.

"The police have been called," she said quietly, her voice steady despite the tension in the room. "They'll send someone shortly."

Eleanor nodded, her eyes vacant, staring into the distance as though Charlotte's spirit lingered just out of reach. William didn't respond. He turned away from the window, his expression unreadable.

Outside, the lake had returned to its unnatural stillness, the morning mist slowly dissipating as the day wore on. But something had shifted. The estate, once a symbol of power and privilege, now seemed haunted by the spectre of its heiress. The gathered staff remained in their small clusters, speaking in low tones as they awaited the arrival of the authorities.

Whispers of foul play began to spread among them. Though Charlotte had always been a solitary figure, there was something unnerving about her death. The stillness of the lake, the untouched grounds around it, the eerie calm that had followed—it didn't feel right. Accidents didn't happen in places like this, and certainly not to people like Charlotte Winthrop.

As the hours passed, the anticipation grew. The authorities would arrive soon, and with them, questions. Questions no one wanted to answer.

And the Winthrops—well, they were a family built on secrets. Secrets that now threatened to come to the surface, just as their heiress had.

But the detective did not come. Not yet.

As the sun climbed higher in the sky, the estate stood in limbo, the tension thick and unyielding. The lake, still and silent once more, held its secrets close, just as it always had.

For now, Charlotte's death remained a mystery. But mysteries, like bodies, never stayed buried for long.

Chapter 2: A Family Affair

The car rumbled up the winding drive, dust swirling in its wake as it approached the towering gates of the Winthrop estate. Detective Jonathan Marlowe tapped his fingers against the steering wheel, his eyes narrowing as the mansion came into view, imposing and untouchable beneath the grey morning sky. It was his first time at the estate, but he had heard about the place for years—everyone had. The Winthrop family wasn't just wealthy, they were old money, the kind that built cities, influenced governments, and carried more power in a single family name than most people could fathom.

But money couldn't protect anyone from death. Not even a Winthrop.

Marlowe's partner, Detective Rachel Suarez, glanced at him from the passenger seat, her sharp eyes taking in the sprawling property. "What do you think?" she asked, her voice casual, but her curiosity obvious. "Accident or something more?"

Marlowe didn't answer right away. He'd read the preliminary report: Charlotte Winthrop, heiress to the Winthrop fortune, found dead in the family's private lake. Drowning, with no initial signs of foul play. Yet something about the case gnawed at him. It wasn't just the prominence of the family. It was the silence surrounding her death. Too quiet. Too composed.

"I don't know yet," Marlowe finally said, his tone even. "But I'd bet this isn't as simple as it looks."

The gates slowly swung open, allowing the car to glide into the estate grounds. Manicured lawns stretched out in every direction, the gardens as pristine as the mansion itself. A handful of police vehicles were already parked near the lake, their lights off, the scene eerily calm despite the gravity of what had happened.

As they approached the house, a uniformed officer directed them to a nearby parking area. Marlowe and Suarez stepped out of the car, the crisp autumn air biting at their faces. The towering facade of the mansion loomed above them, its windows dark and foreboding.

"Detectives," the officer greeted them, tipping his head respectfully. "The family's inside, waiting for you."

Marlowe nodded and gestured for Suarez to follow him. As they walked toward the grand entrance, he couldn't help but feel the weight of the place. The Winthrop name carried history, but history had a way of burying its skeletons deep. He had a feeling today they'd be digging up some of those bones.

Inside the mansion, the air was thick with tension. The large foyer, adorned with marble floors and gilded chandeliers, seemed to echo with a heavy silence. The grandeur of the home did little to mask the unease that permeated the space.

A butler, rigid and proper, led them to a large sitting room where the family had gathered. Marlowe stepped into the room, immediately taking stock of the individuals before him. He had read the brief background on each, but seeing them in person was always different.

At the center of the room sat William Winthrop, the patriarch of the family. His presence was commanding, even as he sat in a stiff armchair, his broad shoulders hunched slightly. His face was an emotionless mask, but his eyes flickered with a cold fire that betrayed his restraint. Dressed in a sharp, dark suit, he was the embodiment of power. A man who was used to controlling everything—and everyone—around him. Except, it seemed, his daughter.

Beside him sat Eleanor Winthrop, his wife. In stark contrast to William, Eleanor looked fragile, her pale skin nearly translucent, her hands trembling slightly as they clutched the edge of her handkerchief. She stared straight ahead, her eyes unfocused, as though she were somewhere far away. Her grief was evident, but there was something else beneath the surface—something darker.

David Winthrop, Charlotte's younger brother, stood near the fireplace, leaning casually against the mantel. His posture suggested nonchalance, but his clenched jaw and tight fists told a different story. His eyes darted around the room, not quite meeting anyone else's gaze. Marlowe noted the tension in the way he stood, as if he were barely holding himself together.

Lastly, there was Margaret Shaw, Charlotte's cousin. She sat apart from the family, her posture stiff and composed, her expression carefully neutral. Unlike the others, her face showed no signs of grief—only a cold, analytical calm that struck Marlowe as odd. He filed it away for later.

"Detectives," William Winthrop said, his deep voice cutting through the silence. "Thank you for coming."

Marlowe nodded, stepping forward. "Mr. Winthrop, Mrs. Winthrop, my condolences for your loss. I'm Detective Marlowe, and this is Detective Suarez. We're here to investigate the circumstances surrounding your daughter's death."

Eleanor's hand flew to her mouth, a soft gasp escaping her as if hearing the words aloud made it more real. William's face remained impassive, but his eyes sharpened as they locked onto Marlowe.

"We were told it was an accident," William said, his tone firm, though there was a question lurking beneath his words.

"At this point, we're still gathering information," Marlowe replied, careful to keep his voice measured. "I understand Charlotte was found early this morning in the lake. Do you mind if we ask a few questions about your daughter and the events leading up to her death?"

A flicker of something crossed William's face—hesitation, perhaps. But he nodded. "Of course."

Suarez took out a notebook, poised to write as Marlowe began. "When was the last time any of you saw Charlotte?"

Eleanor shifted in her seat, her voice barely above a whisper. "Last night... at dinner. Around eight. She said she wasn't feeling well and left the table early." Her eyes, glassy with tears, looked toward the window, as if hoping to catch a glimpse of her daughter's ghost.

"And no one saw her after that?" Marlowe pressed gently.

"No," David interjected, his voice tight. "She kept to herself most of the time. It wasn't unusual for her to retreat to her room or... wherever." There was a bitterness in his tone, something unresolved.

"She'd been... distant lately," Eleanor added, her voice trembling. "More than usual."

"Distant how?" Marlowe asked, noting the subtle shift in the room.

"She wasn't herself," William said sharply, cutting off his wife. "She'd become withdrawn, secretive. I'm not sure why."

"Had anything unusual happened recently that might explain this change in behaviour?" Suarez asked, her eyes flicking toward David, whose expression tightened further.

The family exchanged brief glances, but no one spoke.

After a long moment, Margaret Shaw cleared her throat. "Charlotte was under a lot of pressure. Being the heir to the Winthrop fortune isn't easy." Her tone was carefully neutral, almost detached, but there was an edge to it, as though she knew more than she was letting on.

Marlowe turned his attention to her. "And what sort of pressure are you referring to, Ms. Shaw?"

Margaret gave a small, thin-lipped smile. "The pressure of living up to expectations, of course. The Winthrop legacy is a heavy burden to carry. Some people are stronger than others."

The silence that followed was heavy, loaded with unspoken tension. Marlowe could feel the fractures beneath the surface, the thin veneer of civility barely holding together. This family had secrets—of that he was certain.

"I'd like to take a look at Charlotte's room," Marlowe said, breaking the silence. "Would that be possible?"

William nodded. "The butler can show you the way."

As Marlowe and Suarez prepared to leave the room, he glanced back at the family. The Winthrops sat in their gilded cage of wealth and grief, each of them hiding something behind their carefully composed masks.

This wasn't just an accident. He could feel it in the air—the weight of the secrets, the lies, the tensions that had been festering for years.

And now, those secrets were beginning to surface.

Chapter 3: Secrets Beneath the Surface

The butler led Detective Marlowe and Suarez up the grand staircase, the polished marble echoing with each step as they ascended into the private quarters of the Winthrop family. The house itself was an architectural marvel, its hallways lined with oil paintings of ancestors, their stern eyes following the detectives as they passed. The walls whispered with the weight of history—generations of Winthrops who had lived, loved, and died within these walls. And now, one more.

The butler paused outside a large, ornately carved door at the end of a hallway.

"Miss Charlotte's room," he said in a low voice, his face unreadable. He bowed his head slightly, then stepped aside, allowing Marlowe and Suarez to enter.

Marlowe turned the brass handle and pushed open the door. The room was just as he had expected: luxurious, but cold. Despite its grandeur, the space felt strangely impersonal, as if it had been staged for a magazine cover rather than lived in by an heiress. The decor was pristine—muted greys and creams, delicate lace curtains framing tall windows that overlooked the lake below. Everything was in its place, too perfect, as though untouched by human hands.

But it was Charlotte Winthrop's room. And somewhere beneath the elegance, there were clues to be found.

Suarez moved toward the windows, her sharp gaze sweeping the room, while Marlowe began at the dresser. A large, silver-framed photograph caught his eye—Charlotte, smiling faintly, standing between her parents at a charity gala. She looked poised, every bit the elegant socialite. But her eyes told a different story. There was something distant in them, a hollowness that couldn't be masked by the glamorous facade.

He set the photo aside and opened the top drawer. Inside were neatly folded scarves, gloves, and other accessories. Nothing unusual.

He moved to the vanity, scanning its surface: an assortment of expensive perfumes, delicate jewellery, and cosmetics arranged with precision. Nothing here seemed to indicate that Charlotte's life had been anything other than charmed.

Suarez joined him by the bed, her eyes narrowing as she studied the room. "Looks like a showroom," she muttered. "Nothing out of place."

Marlowe nodded. "Too perfect." He bent down and opened the nightstand drawer. Inside, a stack of papers immediately caught his attention. Letters—handwritten, some in envelopes, others left loose.

He pulled out the stack and thumbed through them. The first few appeared to be innocuous correspondence—thank-you notes, invitations to events, and a letter from a charity Charlotte had supported. But as he flipped further, one letter stood out.

It was handwritten in neat, delicate script, but it wasn't signed. Marlowe scanned the contents:

"I can't keep doing this, Charlotte. You have to understand. The pressure is too much, and I can't pretend everything is fine anymore. This can't stay hidden forever—it's tearing me apart. I don't know what you expect me to do."

Marlowe frowned. The letter was vague, but it was clear that whoever had written it was in distress. The tone hinted at a relationship strained by secrecy. He slipped it into his pocket for later analysis.

Next, he pulled open the bottom drawer of the nightstand. There, beneath a stack of fashion magazines, was a small, leather-bound diary. It was plain, worn around the edges, and the clasp was loose as if it had been opened frequently.

He exchanged a glance with Suarez, then opened the diary. Inside, Charlotte's handwriting filled the pages, her thoughts scrawled in elegant, looping cursive. Marlowe flipped through the pages, noting the progression from idle musings about her day-to-day life to increasingly troubled entries. As he read, it became clear that Charlotte's life was far from the fairytale it appeared to be.

One entry, dated six months ago, caught his attention:

"I can't stand it anymore. Everything is closing in on me. The expectations, the pressure—no one understands what it's like to carry the weight of this family. I feel like I'm suffocating under it all. Sometimes, I wish I could disappear."

Marlowe felt a chill crawl down his spine. He read on, the entries growing more and more disjointed as time passed.

"Mother keeps pushing me to marry someone from the right family, but what does she know about love? She's trapped, just like me. Trapped in this gilded cage, playing the perfect wife, the perfect mother. I won't be like her."

"David's getting worse. His temper is out of control, and Father just pretends everything is fine. But I know what's going on. I know what David's been hiding. I saw him that night, by the lake. I don't know what he was doing, but I'm sure of it—he's involved in something dark."

Marlowe's eyes narrowed. David. The younger brother. The one who had seemed too tense, too defensive during the initial interview. He hadn't said much about his relationship with Charlotte, but now it was clear there had been trouble between them.

He continued reading, flipping to the final entry, dated just days before Charlotte's death:

"I feel like I'm drowning, and no one can save me. Everything is spiralling out of control. There are too many secrets—things I can't talk about, things I can't admit, even to myself. I'm afraid of what's coming. I know something terrible is going to happen. I can feel it."

Marlowe closed the diary, his mind racing. Charlotte had been terrified in the days leading up to her death. She had known something was coming—something she couldn't escape.

He looked up at Suarez, who had been scanning the room as he read. "This wasn't an accident," he said, his voice low but certain.

Suarez nodded. "She was scared of something—maybe someone. We need to dig deeper into her family, her relationships. This place is crawling with secrets."

Marlowe pocketed the diary, knowing it would be crucial to their investigation. "Let's start with David," he said. "There's something she knew about him, something she saw. And if it's connected to her death, we're going to find out."

Before they could leave, Suarez noticed something odd about the bedpost near Charlotte's side. She stepped closer and tapped it lightly. The wood gave a hollow sound, and she quickly realized it was loose. Pulling it gently, she revealed a hidden compartment inside the bedpost. Nestled within was a small, silver locket.

She opened it to reveal two photographs—one of Charlotte, and the other of a man Marlowe didn't recognize. His face was youthful, handsome, but there was a shadow in his eyes, something dangerous.

Marlowe's mind whirled. Who was this man? And why was his photo hidden away in a secret compartment?

"We need to figure out who he is," Marlowe said. "Something tells me Charlotte didn't hide him away for no reason."

As they left the room, the weight of what they had uncovered pressed heavily on Marlowe's mind. The perfect life of the Winthrop heiress was nothing more than a veneer, hiding a storm of secrets beneath the surface. Secrets that were starting to unravel.

And somewhere in those secrets was the key to understanding what had really happened to Charlotte Winthrop.

Chapter 4: The Dark Lake

Detective Marlowe sat in his office, the soft hum of the police station around him barely registering as he stared at the autopsy report in his hands. He had known from the moment he saw Charlotte Winthrop's body that there was something off about her death. The pristine calm of the lake, the absence of any struggle on the shore—it all felt too clean, too deliberate. Now, with the coroner's report in front of him, his suspicions had solid ground.

The door creaked open, and Suarez stepped in, her coat still damp from the drizzle outside. She shook the rain from her hair, her eyes sharp as she walked over to Marlowe's desk. "You've got that look," she said, tossing her bag on the chair. "What did the report say?"

Marlowe exhaled and passed her the folder. "Take a look for yourself."

Suarez flipped through the pages, her brow furrowing as she read. "Cause of death is drowning, but there's more," she muttered, scanning the notes from the medical examiner. "Subdermal bruising on the wrists... as if she was restrained."

"Exactly," Marlowe said. "There's no sign of outward trauma, nothing visible at first glance. But under the surface? She had been held down, or at least grabbed with enough force to leave those marks."

Suarez looked up, her expression darkening. "That's not consistent with an accidental drowning. Someone was there with her."

Marlowe nodded. "And it gets worse. The water in her lungs doesn't match the lake water. It's freshwater, but not from the lake. It's cleaner. Too clean."

Suarez blinked in surprise. "What are you saying? She was drowned somewhere else and then moved?"

"That's exactly what the report suggests," Marlowe said, his voice grim. "The coroner's conclusion is that Charlotte was likely drowned in clean, fresh water—like a bathtub, or an indoor pool—before her body was placed in the lake."

The realization settled over them like a heavy fog. Someone had gone through a lot of trouble to stage Charlotte's death as a drowning accident. But why? And more importantly, who?

Marlowe leaned back in his chair, rubbing his temples as his mind raced. "This changes everything. Whoever did this wanted it to look like she drowned naturally, but the bruising and the water in her lungs point to foul play. Someone held her down and made sure she didn't survive."

Suarez closed the file, her eyes narrowing as she pieced the implications together. "The lake was just a cover. They wanted it to look like an accident, but it was staged. This was murder."

Later that afternoon, Marlowe and Suarez returned to the estate, the weight of the new revelations heavy on their shoulders. The overcast sky hung low, casting a pallor over the lake, which now seemed darker, more foreboding. The water's surface, once still and serene, now seemed to ripple with secrets, as though the lake itself knew what had happened to Charlotte.

Marlowe stared out at the water from the shore, his hands in his pockets. The lake had been a symbol of the Winthrop family's wealth and prestige for generations, a place of peace and privacy. Now it had become something else entirely—a crime scene.

"They went through a lot of trouble to make it look like an accident," Suarez said, standing beside him. "Why bother? If someone wanted her dead, why not just make it look like a robbery gone wrong, or a simple disappearance?"

Marlowe considered her words carefully. "The Winthrop name carries weight. A scandalous death, especially murder, would attract too much attention. Whoever did this wanted to minimize the fallout. An accident—especially one involving the family's private lake—could be passed off quietly. Less public scrutiny."

"And yet," Suarez said, kicking a small stone into the water, "they didn't account for the bruising or the water in her lungs. They weren't careful enough."

"Or maybe they didn't expect us to look that closely," Marlowe muttered. "They were banking on the family's influence to keep things under wraps. If we weren't as thorough, we might've written it off as an accident."

Suarez shook her head. "But why would Charlotte's own family want her dead? It doesn't make sense."

Marlowe's eyes narrowed as he looked back at the mansion. "We know there were tensions in that family. The diary we found in her room mentioned David—she was afraid of him. And there's still the matter of that letter she received from someone who was clearly under a lot of pressure. If she knew something—something that threatened the family's reputation or their fortune—someone might've decided she was too much of a risk."

Back inside the mansion, the air was thick with tension. Eleanor Winthrop sat in the drawing room, her posture rigid, as though she were holding herself together by sheer will. David lounged near the window, his eyes darting nervously between Marlowe and Suarez as they stood before him.

"We've received the autopsy report," Marlowe began, his tone neutral but firm. "It confirms what we feared. Charlotte didn't drown by accident. She was killed."

Eleanor gasped, her hand flying to her mouth. "Killed?" she whispered, her voice trembling. "But... how?"

David's expression hardened, though he said nothing, his hands gripping the edge of the windowsill.

"The report shows signs of struggle," Suarez continued. "Bruising on her wrists, suggesting she was restrained. And the water in her lungs doesn't match the lake."

Eleanor's eyes filled with tears, her face going pale. "I... I can't believe it."

But David remained silent, his body tense, his gaze fixed on the floor.

Marlowe stepped forward, his voice steady. "David, you and Charlotte had a complicated relationship. Your sister's diary suggests that there was tension between the two of you. She mentioned seeing you near the lake one night. What were you doing there?"

David's head snapped up, his face flushed with anger. "What are you suggesting?" he demanded, his voice rising. "That I killed my own sister? That's ridiculous!"

"No one's accusing you yet," Marlowe said evenly, "but we need answers. You were one of the last people to see her alive. We need to know what happened between you and Charlotte."

David took a step toward Marlowe, his fists clenched. "Charlotte was a mess! She wasn't herself these past few months. She kept to herself, always secretive, always hiding something. I tried to talk to her, to help her, but she wouldn't listen! And now you're standing here, accusing me of... what? Murder?"

Eleanor sobbed quietly in the background, her fragile composure finally crumbling under the weight of her son's outburst.

Marlowe remained calm, his gaze steady. "No one's accusing you—yet. But if you have nothing to hide, you'll cooperate with the investigation. We need to find out what really happened to your sister."

David glared at him for a moment longer before storming out of the room, his footsteps echoing down the hall.

Suarez glanced at Marlowe, her expression unreadable. "He's hiding something," she whispered.

Marlowe nodded. "And we're going to find out what."

As they left the drawing room, the weight of the case pressed down on them both. The lake had given them their first real clues, but it also deepened the mystery. Someone had gone to great lengths to cover up Charlotte's murder. Now, they had to uncover not only the killer's identity, but the motives behind it. And with every step closer to the truth, it became clear: this family was far more dangerous than they appeared.

The dark lake had concealed Charlotte's body, but it couldn't hide the secrets that were now beginning to rise to the surface.

Chapter 5: The Family Patriarch

Detective Jonathan Marlowe stepped into the dimly lit study of William Winthrop, the patriarch of the family whose name carried as much weight as it did shadow. The study was a monument to the past—a room filled with the smell of old leather and polished wood, the shelves lined with legal tomes and first-edition classics that hadn't been touched in years. A fire crackled softly in the hearth, casting flickering shadows on the walls, but the warmth did little to dispel the chill that hung in the air.

At the far end of the room, behind a massive mahogany desk, sat William Winthrop. His back was straight, his hands clasped on the desk in front of him, and his eyes fixed somewhere beyond the detective as though he were staring down an invisible adversary. He was a man who exuded control—a man who expected the world to bend to his will. But today, that control seemed tenuous, the lines of tension on his face betraying what his cold demeanour sought to hide.

Marlowe closed the door quietly behind him and approached the desk. "Mr. Winthrop," he greeted, keeping his voice neutral. "Thank you for agreeing to speak with me."

William's gaze finally shifted to Marlowe, his eyes as hard as the wood beneath his fingers. He nodded once, a brief acknowledgment, but said nothing.

Marlowe took a seat across from him, aware that this was no ordinary conversation. This was a duel, one that William Winthrop had likely played many times before in boardrooms and legal battles. The man wasn't just wealthy; he was powerful. And in his world, power meant silence could speak louder than words.

"I know this is a difficult time for you," Marlowe began, carefully choosing his words. "Your daughter's death has left a lot of unanswered questions, and my job is to find those answers."

William's lips tightened ever so slightly. "You've already spoken with my wife, my son, and other members of the family. I'm not sure what more I can tell you, Detective."

His tone was even, devoid of emotion. A perfectly measured response. Marlowe wasn't surprised.

"With all due respect, Mr. Winthrop, I believe you know more than you're letting on," Marlowe said, leaning forward slightly. "You had a complicated relationship with Charlotte, didn't you?"

William's jaw clenched, but he remained silent for a long moment. Then, finally, he spoke, his voice low and controlled. "Charlotte was my daughter. My only daughter. I did everything I could to provide for her, to give her the life she deserved."

Marlowe nodded, but he could feel the tension simmering beneath the man's composed exterior. "And yet, she struggled. She felt trapped by the expectations placed on her—expectations that, from what I understand, you set."

William's eyes flashed, a brief flicker of anger breaking through the icy facade. "Do not presume to understand my family, Detective," he said, his voice now edged with steel. "Charlotte was born into privilege, into a world that most people can only dream of. She had every opportunity, every advantage. If she chose not to embrace them, that was her decision."

Marlowe held William's gaze, refusing to back down. "And what about the pressure she was under? The pressure to uphold the family legacy? She felt like she was suffocating under it."

William's expression didn't change, but his silence spoke volumes. For a man who prided himself on control, on managing every detail of his life and his family's, the idea that his daughter had slipped through his fingers—had struggled beneath the weight of the very legacy he had worked so hard to build—must have felt like failure.

Marlowe decided to push further. "I read her diary, Mr. Winthrop. She was deeply troubled in the months leading up to her death. She was afraid. She mentioned seeing David by the lake one night. She believed something was going on. Did you know about that?"

For the first time, William's mask slipped, if only for a second. His eyes narrowed, a flicker of something—fear? Anger?—flashing across his face. "David is my son. Whatever differences they may have had, it is not relevant to what happened to Charlotte."

"Isn't it?" Marlowe pressed. "You've built an empire, Mr. Winthrop, and it's clear you'll do anything to protect it. But your daughter was suffering, and someone in this family—maybe more than one person—had something to hide. Why haven't you cooperated more fully with this investigation?"

William's fingers tightened on the edge of the desk, his knuckles whitening. His voice dropped to a low, dangerous tone. "Detective, I understand that you have a job to do. But if you're suggesting that I had something to do with my daughter's death, you are gravely mistaken."

Marlowe didn't flinch. "I'm not accusing you, Mr. Winthrop. But I am saying that your silence raises questions. You control everything around you. And yet, when it comes to your daughter's death, you've barely said a word. You haven't expressed any outrage, any demand for justice. Why?"

William's eyes burned with cold fire now, but his voice remained calm, calculated. "I grieve for Charlotte in my own way. My family's affairs are our own. The police may investigate, but I will not have our private matters paraded around for the world to see. This family has endured enough."

Marlowe studied him, sensing that he was hitting a nerve but also realizing that William was a fortress. The man had spent decades building walls, mastering the art of control. Breaking through that wall would take more than a direct assault.

He decided to change tactics. "Your daughter was killed, Mr. Winthrop," he said quietly, letting the weight of the words hang in the air. "And whoever did this went to great lengths to make it look like an accident. But it wasn't an accident. I think you know that. The question is, what are you willing to do about it?"

For a long moment, William said nothing. His face was unreadable, his gaze fixed on some distant point behind Marlowe's shoulder. Then, finally, he spoke, his voice as cold and distant as ever.

"Charlotte made choices," he said slowly, deliberately. "Some of those choices were not ones I would have made. But that was her right as an adult. My role as her father was to guide her, to protect her where I could. But in the end, we are all responsible for our own lives."

Marlowe frowned, unsure if William was speaking in code, hiding something deeper in his words, or if this was just another layer of detachment. "And what choices are you referring to? What was Charlotte involved in that you didn't approve of?"

William's gaze sharpened, the cold fire returning. "That is not your concern, Detective. Charlotte's choices were her own, and they died with her."

The words hung in the air like a final, unyielding statement, an impenetrable wall that Marlowe knew he wouldn't breach today. William Winthrop wasn't going to give him anything. At least not yet.

Marlowe stood, knowing that any further questioning would only be met with the same stonewalling. "We'll continue our investigation, Mr. Winthrop," he said evenly. "If you remember anything—or if you choose to be more forthcoming—let us know."

William didn't respond, simply turning his gaze back to the fire as Marlowe made his way toward the door. As the detective reached for the handle, William spoke again, his voice barely above a whisper.

"Find whoever did this, Detective. But be careful what you uncover. Some things are better left buried."

Marlowe paused, the weight of the words settling on his shoulders. There was more to this than William was willing to admit. The patriarch of the Winthrop family was a man of silence, but that silence spoke volumes.

As Marlowe stepped out into the hallway, the fire in the study continued to crackle softly behind him. The patriarch remained at his desk, alone, as the shadows danced on the walls—a powerful man, but one haunted by the secrets of his own making.

Chapter 6: Mother's Grief

The sitting room was quiet, save for the soft ticking of a grandfather clock against the far wall. The muted afternoon light filtered through the heavy curtains, casting long shadows across the dark oak furniture. Eleanor Winthrop sat on a plush settee, her pale hands folded in her lap, trembling slightly as she stared down at the floor. She was the picture of grief—fragile, exhausted, her face etched with sorrow—but to Detective Marlowe, something about her grief felt distant, almost rehearsed.

Marlowe watched her carefully as he took a seat across from her, his notebook resting in his lap. The air in the room was thick with tension, though Eleanor seemed barely present, her mind drifting somewhere far beyond the walls of the mansion. Her thin frame, clad in a dark, conservative dress, seemed to shrink into the upholstery, as if she could disappear into the fabric if she tried hard enough.

"Mrs. Winthrop," Marlowe began softly, his voice low and soothing, "I know this is an incredibly difficult time for you, but I need to ask you a few questions about the night Charlotte died. Can you walk me through that evening again?"

Eleanor looked up at him, her eyes glassy and rimmed with red. She blinked, as if coming out of a fog, and nodded slowly. "Yes... yes, of course," she murmured, her voice barely audible.

She took a deep breath, her gaze unfocused as she began to speak. "It was a quiet night. Charlotte... she wasn't feeling well. She mentioned a headache during dinner and left the table early. That was the last time I saw her." Her voice faltered, and she dabbed at her eyes with a lace handkerchief. "She said she was going to her room to rest. I didn't think anything of it... I never imagined..." Her words trailed off into silence.

Marlowe waited a moment before continuing. "You said you didn't see her again after she left the dinner table. What time was that?"

Eleanor furrowed her brow, as if struggling to recall. "I think... it must have been around eight. Yes, just after eight."

Marlowe scribbled the detail in his notebook. "And did you hear anything unusual later that night? Any noises? Did Charlotte say anything before she left the room?"

Eleanor hesitated, her fingers gripping the handkerchief tightly. "No... I mean, I don't remember. The house is so large, you don't always hear everything." She looked up at him, her eyes wide and pleading. "She was quiet, you see? Always so quiet. She didn't want to be a burden."

Marlowe nodded, but something about her hesitation tugged at him. Her grief seemed genuine, but it was as if she was choosing her words carefully, her thoughts clouded by more than just sadness. He leaned forward slightly, his voice still gentle but probing. "Mrs. Winthrop, I need to ask—are you sure you didn't hear or see anything after Charlotte went to her room? Perhaps later in the evening?"

Eleanor blinked rapidly, her hands twisting the handkerchief in her lap. "I... I don't know," she stammered. "I went to bed early. I wasn't feeling well either. I didn't hear anything."

Marlowe studied her for a moment before speaking again. "Mrs. Winthrop, the night your daughter died, did you leave your room at all after dinner?"

She flinched, her eyes darting toward the window as though searching for an escape. "No, I... I was in my room the whole night," she said quickly. Too quickly. "I didn't leave."

Marlowe caught the hesitation, the subtle tremor in her voice. "Are you certain? It's important that we have an accurate timeline."

Eleanor's grip on the handkerchief tightened, her knuckles turning white. "Yes," she said more firmly. "I didn't leave my room."

Marlowe nodded, though his instincts told him she wasn't being entirely truthful. There was something she wasn't saying. He decided to shift the conversation, hoping to uncover what she might be hiding.

"Charlotte's diary mentioned that she was feeling a lot of pressure lately," Marlowe said carefully. "Pressure from the family, from expectations. She seemed very troubled. Did she ever talk to you about what was bothering her?"

Eleanor's eyes welled with tears again, and she shook her head slowly. "No... Charlotte was always so private. She never wanted to worry me." Her voice cracked, and she pressed the handkerchief to her mouth, as if to stifle a sob. "But I knew... I knew she was struggling."

Marlowe felt the shift—this was where the truth might begin to leak through the cracks. "What was she struggling with, Mrs. Winthrop? Was there something specific she was afraid of? Someone she was afraid of?"

Eleanor's tears spilled over, and she turned her face away, staring at the fire as if the flames held the answers. "She... she felt trapped," she whispered. "Trapped by the expectations, by the family. William... her father... he had so many plans for her. She never wanted to disappoint him."

Marlowe's interest piqued. "Plans? What kind of plans?"

Eleanor wiped her eyes, her voice shaky. "He... wanted her to marry well. To keep the family legacy intact. There were discussions, arrangements with families in our social circle. She didn't want any part of it."

Marlowe leaned forward. "Were these arrangements something Charlotte actively resisted?"

Eleanor nodded, her gaze still distant. "Yes... she resisted. She wanted to live her own life. But William... he wouldn't hear of it. He thought she was being foolish, that she didn't understand her responsibilities to the family."

Marlowe scribbled notes in his book, the picture becoming clearer. Charlotte had felt suffocated by the weight of her family's expectations, her father's control over her future. "Did Charlotte ever talk about leaving? About escaping from the family's control?"

For the briefest moment, Eleanor's face tightened, and she hesitated again. "Yes," she whispered, almost inaudibly. "She talked about leaving... starting over somewhere far away. But it was just talk. Charlotte was too loyal to her family, despite everything. She couldn't bring herself to leave us."

There was a long silence as Marlowe digested this. He shifted slightly in his chair before continuing. "Mrs. Winthrop, I need to ask you about the night Charlotte was found. The staff mentioned that you seemed... distraught, but also hesitant to come outside when they discovered her body. Can you tell me why?"

Eleanor's face paled, and her hands began to tremble even more. "I... I was in shock. I didn't... I couldn't..." Her voice broke, and she covered her face with her hands.

Marlowe waited patiently. When she didn't continue, he spoke softly, "Mrs. Winthrop, I understand this is difficult. But your reaction that night seemed unusual. You didn't leave your room immediately when they found her, and when you did, you seemed... distant."

She lifted her head, her face streaked with tears. "I was scared," she whispered. "I didn't want to see her like that. My baby... I couldn't bear it."

Marlowe studied her carefully. There was something in her expression, something that hinted at more than just fear. Guilt. But guilt over what?

"Mrs. Winthrop, is there something you haven't told me?" he asked quietly, his tone soft but insistent. "Something you're afraid to share?"

Eleanor's breath hitched, and for a moment, he thought she might break down completely. But instead, she composed herself, wiping her eyes and sitting up straighter. "No, Detective. There's nothing more. I told you everything I know."

Marlowe didn't believe her. But he knew pushing too hard now wouldn't get him anywhere. Eleanor Winthrop was a woman steeped in grief, but there was more to her sadness than the loss of her daughter.

There were secrets buried deep in this family—secrets that Charlotte had tried to escape, and secrets that her mother was still trying to protect.

As Marlowe stood to leave, he glanced once more at Eleanor. Her gaze had returned to the fire, her expression blank. She had said enough to give him new leads, but she had also held back, guarding the family's most dangerous truths.

"Thank you for your time, Mrs. Winthrop," he said quietly.

Eleanor nodded but didn't speak, her eyes fixed on the flames as if hoping they might consume everything she wished she could forget.

Marlowe left the room, the soft click of the door closing behind him barely audible over the steady ticking of the clock. Outside, the mansion's halls were quiet, but the echoes of long-hidden secrets lingered in the air, growing louder with every step he took.

Chapter 7: Sibling Rivalry

Detective Marlowe found David Winthrop sitting on the stone steps at the back of the mansion, facing the lake where his sister's body had been found. The overcast sky cast a dull, muted light over the scene, and the still waters reflected the heavy clouds overhead. The wind rustled the nearby trees, but David remained unmoving, his face a mask of unreadable emotions as he stared out at the water.

Marlowe approached slowly, taking in the younger Winthrop's rigid posture and clenched fists. David was the image of a man tightly wound, barely holding his emotions in check. His dishevelled hair and the dark circles under his eyes told Marlowe this was a man who hadn't slept well in days—perhaps longer.

"David," Marlowe called out as he neared. "Do you mind if I sit with you?"

David barely glanced at him, his eyes never leaving the lake. "I don't see the point," he muttered, his voice low and strained. "You're going to ask the same damn questions everyone else has asked."

Marlowe remained standing for a moment, studying David's profile. There was anger there—anger and something deeper, something darker. Finally, Marlowe sat down beside him, keeping a respectful distance but close enough to show he wasn't going anywhere until they talked.

"I'm not here to waste your time," Marlowe said evenly. "But I do need to understand what happened between you and your sister."

David's jaw tightened at the mention of Charlotte, but he didn't respond right away. He ran a hand through his hair, exhaling sharply. "Everyone keeps acting like she was some perfect little princess. But she wasn't. Not to me, anyway."

Marlowe raised an eyebrow, sensing the first crack in David's carefully maintained facade. "What do you mean by that?"

David let out a bitter laugh, though it held no warmth. "She was the golden child. Everyone knew it. My father made sure of that. Charlotte could do no wrong in his eyes. Everything revolved around her—the family business, the inheritance, the expectations. I was just... the spare."

Marlowe noted the bitterness in his voice, the resentment that simmered just beneath the surface. "That must've been difficult."

David scoffed. "Difficult? It was infuriating. I was constantly reminded that I wasn't important, that my life didn't matter as much as hers. Charlotte was being groomed to take over the family empire, and I was... well, I was left to fend for myself."

The tension in David's voice was palpable now, his words clipped and sharp. Marlowe let the silence hang for a moment before pushing gently. "But you weren't just siblings. You were family. Surely you and Charlotte had moments where you were close, where you supported each other."

David's eyes flashed with anger as he turned to face Marlowe for the first time. "Close?" he repeated incredulously. "We were never close. Charlotte never gave a damn about me. All she cared about was her own life—her own problems. She never once considered how any of this affected me."

Marlowe held David's gaze, sensing the raw pain in his words. "What kind of problems are we talking about?"

David looked away, staring at the lake again, but his expression darkened. "She was always so secretive, like she had the world on her shoulders. But she didn't share anything with me—not really. She acted like I couldn't possibly understand what she was going through. Like I was beneath her."

There it was—jealousy, plain and simple. Marlowe could hear it in every syllable. But this wasn't just petty sibling rivalry. It ran deeper than that, like a wound that had festered for years, untreated.

"Did that ever make you angry?" Marlowe asked, his voice calm but probing.

David's mouth twisted into a bitter smile. "Of course it did. I spent my whole life in her shadow. Nothing I ever did was good enough because it was always compared to her. And then, just when I thought maybe I could finally break free, she'd come back into the picture, and it was like everything revolved around her again."

Marlowe leaned forward slightly. "What happened the night she died? Did you see her?"

David's expression shifted, the tension in his body tightening even further. "I saw her earlier that evening, yeah. We had dinner together, the whole family. But she left early, like she always did. I didn't see her after that."

Marlowe's instincts told him there was more to the story. He decided to press a little harder. "Your sister's diary mentioned seeing you by the lake one night. She was concerned about what you were involved in. Why would she be worried about you?"

David's eyes narrowed, and his face darkened with anger. "Charlotte didn't know what she was talking about," he snapped. "She always thought she was so much better than me—like she had all the answers. But she didn't know anything about my life."

"What were you doing by the lake that night?" Marlowe asked, his voice steady.

David stood up suddenly, the movement abrupt and filled with pent-up energy. "That's none of your business," he said coldly, pacing along the edge of the stone steps. "I don't owe you any explanations."

Marlowe watched him carefully, noting how agitated he had become. David was clearly hiding something, something that had to do with that night. "I'm not here to accuse you, David. But if you were involved in anything that might have affected your sister—whether directly or indirectly—I need to know. This is about finding the truth."

David stopped pacing, his shoulders heaving as he tried to rein in his emotions. He turned to face Marlowe, his eyes filled with a mix of anger and something else—fear. "You think I had something to do with this, don't you? You think I killed her."

Marlowe remained seated, his gaze steady. "I don't know what happened yet. But I do know that there was tension between you and Charlotte, and that tension might've led to something neither of you could control."

David clenched his fists, his knuckles white. "I didn't kill her," he said through gritted teeth. "I may have hated the way things were between us, but I would never hurt her. She was my sister."

Marlowe didn't flinch. "Then help me understand what did happen. Why was Charlotte so worried about you? What were you doing that night?"

David was silent for a long moment, his face twisted with indecision. Finally, he let out a heavy sigh, the fight draining out of him. "It was about the money," he muttered, his voice barely above a whisper. "The inheritance. Charlotte was supposed to get most of it. But I found out something—something that could've changed everything."

Marlowe's interest piqued. "What did you find out?"

David swallowed hard, his gaze flickering nervously toward the mansion as if he were afraid of being overheard. "There were conditions to the inheritance—stipulations in the will that my father never told us about. If certain things happened, the money would be split differently. I... I thought I could use that to my advantage."

Marlowe's eyes narrowed. "What kind of conditions?"

David hesitated, then shook his head. "I don't know all the details. But I overheard my father talking to the lawyer about it. Something about controlling shares in the family business, and how Charlotte's decisions could impact the future of the estate. I thought if I could convince her to leave, or if she did something that broke those conditions... maybe I'd get what was mine."

Marlowe felt the pieces beginning to come together. David's jealousy, his bitterness over being overshadowed by his sister, and now the financial stakes—it all pointed to motive. But there was still one question hanging in the air.

"Did you confront her about it?" Marlowe asked.

David's face hardened again. "I tried to talk to her. But she wouldn't listen. She never listened to me. She said I was being selfish, that I was obsessed with the money. And maybe I was... but I didn't want her dead."

Marlowe studied David's face, searching for any sign of deception. The young man was clearly angry, bitter, and perhaps even desperate. But was he telling the truth?

As the silence stretched between them, Marlowe stood and met David's gaze head-on. "I need to know everything, David. If there's more you're not telling me, now's the time."

David's shoulders slumped, and he shook his head, defeated. "I've told you everything I know. I didn't kill her."

Marlowe nodded, though he wasn't entirely convinced. There were still gaps in David's story—gaps that could only be filled with more digging.

As Marlowe walked back toward the mansion, leaving David standing by the lake, he couldn't shake the feeling that this family's secrets were far more tangled than he'd realized. And with every new revelation, the list of potential suspects grew longer.

Sibling rivalry was one thing. But in the Winthrop family, rivalry had turned deadly.

Chapter 8: The Lover

Detective Jonathan Marlowe sat in his office, the soft buzz of the station's activity humming in the background. In front of him lay a file that had come in earlier that morning—something unexpected. The results from a search through Charlotte Winthrop's personal records had revealed a phone number that didn't match any of her known contacts. The number had been called repeatedly in the weeks leading up to her death. It was curious enough to warrant further investigation.

His instinct told him this could be significant. Charlotte's relationships with her family had been tense, and she'd hidden much of her personal life from them. But this number, frequent calls to an unknown recipient, hinted at something she had kept not only from her family, but from the world. A relationship, perhaps.

Marlowe picked up the phone and dialled the number. After a few rings, a man's voice answered, slightly wary. "Hello?"

Marlowe kept his tone neutral. "This is Detective Jonathan Marlowe with the police department. May I ask who I'm speaking to?"

There was a pause on the other end, then the man responded, his voice now more guarded. "This is Mark Hayes. What's this about?"

Marlowe scribbled the name down. It didn't ring any immediate bells, but that didn't matter. "Mr. Hayes, I'm investigating the death of Charlotte Winthrop, and your number came up in connection with her phone records. I'd like to ask you a few questions."

There was a long silence, and Marlowe could almost feel the tension crackling through the line. Finally, Mark spoke, his voice tight. "I'm not sure how I can help with that."

Marlowe leaned forward in his chair. "I think you can help more than you realize, Mr. Hayes. According to these records, you were in contact with Charlotte frequently. I assume the two of you knew each other well?"

Mark sighed, the sound heavy with resignation. "Yeah... we knew each other. But I didn't want to get involved in all of this."

Marlowe's senses sharpened. There was something in that statement—something more than reluctance. "What do you mean by 'get involved'?" he asked, his voice even but probing.

"I don't want trouble, Detective. I didn't have anything to do with what happened to her," Mark said quickly, as if trying to pre-empt the line of questioning. "But... we were seeing each other. In secret."

There it was. Marlowe felt a jolt of anticipation. "Seeing each other? You were in a relationship?"

"Yes," Mark admitted after a beat. "But no one knew about it. Charlotte didn't want her family to find out. She said they wouldn't understand."

Marlowe leaned back in his chair, processing the information. A hidden relationship—one Charlotte had gone to great lengths to keep from her powerful family. That alone made this Mark Hayes a person of interest. "How long had you been seeing each other?" Marlowe asked, his tone steady but pointed.

"About six months," Mark said, his voice quieter now. "We met at a charity event I was working at. I'm a photographer, and I was covering the event. We hit it off and started seeing each other soon after."

Marlowe scribbled down notes. "Did Charlotte ever talk about her family? Specifically, any trouble she was having with them?"

Mark hesitated before answering. "She didn't like talking about them much. She was under a lot of pressure—especially from her father. She hated the expectations, the way she was supposed to fit into this perfect little box they'd built for her. But she couldn't break free."

"And how did that make her feel?" Marlowe asked, pushing deeper.

"She felt trapped," Mark replied, his voice now laced with emotion. "She talked about leaving sometimes. About running away, starting fresh somewhere far from here. But... she always came back to them. It was like she couldn't really escape, no matter how much she wanted to."

Marlowe frowned, his mind racing. This fit with what he had learned so far about Charlotte's strained relationship with her family. But there was still more to uncover. "When was the last time you saw her, Mr. Hayes?"

There was a pause. "Two days before she died. She came over to my place. She seemed... tense, more than usual. She was scared, I think. She wouldn't say exactly what was bothering her, but I could tell something was wrong. She kept looking over her shoulder, like she thought someone was watching her."

Marlowe's interest piqued. "Did she mention who she was afraid of?"

"No," Mark said quickly. "But she did mention her father a few times—how controlling he was. She said there were things she couldn't tell me, things about her family that she didn't even want to think about."

Marlowe felt the pieces falling into place. Charlotte had been keeping secrets—secrets about her family that had likely contributed to her fear and paranoia in the days leading up to her death. "Did Charlotte say anything specific about what she was planning to do? Did she intend to confront anyone?"

Mark hesitated. "She said she had to make a decision soon. She didn't say what it was about, but she kept saying she was running out of time."

Running out of time. Marlowe jotted down the phrase. What had Charlotte been so afraid of? And more importantly, what decision had she been struggling with?

"Mark," Marlowe said, his tone shifting slightly, "you understand that this makes you a person of interest, don't you? You were involved with Charlotte, and no one else knew about it. I need to know where you were the night she died."

"I had nothing to do with her death," Mark said quickly, his voice defensive. "I wasn't even near the estate that night. I was at a photo shoot in the city, and you can check with the people I was working with. They'll confirm it."

Marlowe scribbled the information down. It wasn't a confession, but the fact that Mark had an alibi was important. Still, he couldn't shake the feeling that there was more Mark wasn't telling him. "I'll need the names of the people you were with," Marlowe said.

Mark sighed heavily, the exhaustion in his voice unmistakable. "I'll give you the information, Detective. But please... I didn't hurt her. I loved her. I wanted to help her, but she was... caught up in something bigger than either of us."

Marlowe nodded, though he wasn't ready to let go of his suspicions. "One last question, Mark. Did Charlotte mention anyone else? Someone who might have been threatening her or trying to manipulate her?"

Mark was silent for a moment, then he spoke, his voice barely a whisper. "There was someone... I don't know who. But she got a phone call one night, late. I heard her arguing with someone—she was angry, but scared, too. She didn't tell me who it was, but she said they had 'the power to ruin everything.'"

Marlowe's pulse quickened. This was it—a lead. Someone had been pressuring Charlotte, someone with enough influence to terrify her. And now that person might be responsible for her death.

"I'll be in touch, Mr. Hayes," Marlowe said, his voice firm. "And thank you for your cooperation."

As he hung up the phone, Marlowe stared at the notes in front of him. Charlotte's secret lover, hidden from her powerful family, had been one part of her life she'd tried to keep under control. But there was another shadow—someone who had been pulling strings behind the scenes, someone with the power to "ruin everything."

Marlowe knew that finding this person would be key to solving the mystery of Charlotte Winthrop's death.

And the clock was ticking.

Chapter 9: The Housekeeper's Confession

Detective Marlowe walked through the grand halls of the Winthrop estate, the echoes of his footsteps bouncing off the marble floors. The opulence of the mansion was undeniable, but after days of investigating the family, he knew that beneath the glittering surface was a festering mess of secrets. As he made his way toward the servants' quarters, he felt the tension of the house pressing in on him—this was a place where appearances were everything, and no one was who they seemed.

The housekeeper, Mrs. Iris Cunningham, had been with the Winthrop family for over three decades. She knew the rhythms of the house better than anyone. But like most longtime employees of the wealthy, she had remained tight-lipped about the internal affairs of her employers—until now. Earlier that morning, Marlowe had received word that she was ready to talk, though what had changed her mind remained a mystery. Still, Marlowe could sense the tide turning. With every interview, every new piece of information, the threads of the Winthrop family's dysfunction were slowly unravelling.

Marlowe knocked gently on the door of Mrs. Cunningham's modest office. The room was small, furnished simply with a desk, a chair, and a few old photographs on the wall. When the door opened, the housekeeper stood before him, her hands clasped tightly in front of her apron, her face a mixture of apprehension and weariness.

"Detective," she greeted softly. Her voice was low, as though she feared being overheard.

"Mrs. Cunningham," Marlowe said, offering a kind nod as he stepped into the room. "Thank you for agreeing to speak with me."

Mrs. Cunningham motioned toward the chair across from her desk. "Please, sit."

Marlowe took his seat, observing the older woman as she moved behind her desk. She was composed, but there was a tremor in her hands as she settled into the chair. Her grey hair was neatly pulled back, and her uniform was immaculate, but her eyes betrayed a deep sadness—perhaps even guilt.

"I've worked for this family for a long time, Detective," she began without preamble. "I've seen a lot. Heard a lot." She paused, her lips tightening. "But I've always kept my place. It's not my role to get involved in the family's affairs."

Marlowe leaned forward slightly, his tone gentle but firm. "I understand, Mrs. Cunningham. But you also know that Charlotte is dead, and this family is in turmoil. If there's something you know—something you've heard—it could help us find out what really happened to her."

Mrs. Cunningham's eyes flickered with uncertainty, but then she nodded slowly, as though coming to a decision. "I couldn't hold it in any longer. Not after what I heard before she died."

Marlowe's pulse quickened. "What did you hear?"

Mrs. Cunningham took a deep breath, her fingers twisting the fabric of her apron. "There were arguments. Charlotte and her father... they fought a lot in the last few months. I overheard one of those arguments—late at night, just a few days before she... before they found her in the lake."

Marlowe's brows furrowed. "What were they arguing about?"

"It was always the same thing," Mrs. Cunningham said, her voice lowering. "The inheritance. Mr. Winthrop had plans for Charlotte—he wanted her to follow in his footsteps, take control of the family business. But Charlotte... she wanted none of it. She told him she was leaving, that she couldn't live like this anymore."

"Leaving?" Marlowe asked, his mind racing back to what Mark Hayes had told him. Charlotte had mentioned leaving, running away from her family's control. "Did she say where she planned to go?"

Mrs. Cunningham shook her head. "She didn't say. But she was adamant. She told Mr. Winthrop she was done being his puppet. That she was tired of living her life according to his plans."

Marlowe scribbled in his notebook, his suspicions about William Winthrop deepening. "How did her father react?"

The housekeeper hesitated, her voice trembling. "He... he didn't take it well. I heard him shouting at her. He said she was being foolish, that she didn't understand the consequences of her actions. He said she had responsibilities to the family, to the legacy. But Charlotte... she stood her ground."

Marlowe nodded slowly. "And was there anyone else present during these arguments? Did anyone else witness what happened?"

Mrs. Cunningham pursed her lips. "Not during that argument, no. But I've heard other things, over time. There's always been tension between the siblings. David and Charlotte—there was rivalry between them, always. Mr. Winthrop favoured Charlotte for the business, but David... he resented her for it. I've seen them argue, too. Sometimes over money, sometimes over their father's plans for them."

Marlowe leaned forward, pressing gently. "Did you hear anything specific between David and Charlotte? Anything that could suggest why things were so strained between them?"

The housekeeper's eyes darted toward the door, as though she feared someone might be listening in. Then she whispered, "There was one night... about a month ago. I was cleaning the hallway outside the library, and I heard them. David and Charlotte. They were shouting at each other. I couldn't hear everything, but I caught bits and pieces. Charlotte was accusing David of something—she said she knew about his 'deal' with someone, that he was trying to undermine her."

Marlowe's heart skipped a beat. "Undermine her? Did she say what kind of deal it was?"

"No," Mrs. Cunningham replied, shaking her head. "But whatever it was, it sounded serious. David was furious. He told her to stay out of his business, that she didn't know what she was talking about. They were both so angry."

Marlowe made a mental note of the confrontation. David had already admitted to harbouring resentment toward his sister, but if he had been involved in something shady—something Charlotte had found out about—then that could have been a motive for wanting her silenced.

"Did Charlotte ever confide in you directly, Mrs. Cunningham?" Marlowe asked. "Did she say anything about her fears, or about what she was planning?"

The housekeeper's eyes filled with sadness, and she shook her head. "No, Detective. Charlotte didn't talk to me about her personal life. She was always kind, but distant. I think… she was very lonely. For all the wealth and power her family had, she didn't have anyone she could truly trust."

Marlowe nodded, absorbing the weight of the housekeeper's words. "Is there anything else you remember hearing? Anything that might help us understand what Charlotte was dealing with before she died?"

Mrs. Cunningham hesitated, her hands trembling slightly. "There is one more thing," she whispered. "The night before she died… I heard her talking on the phone. I was passing by her room, and the door was slightly ajar. She was upset, crying. She kept saying, 'I can't do this anymore. I won't be part of this.' She didn't say who she was talking to, but it sounded like she was afraid."

Marlowe's eyes narrowed. "Did she mention a name?"

"No," the housekeeper replied. "But she was clearly distressed. And then, the next morning, she was gone."

Marlowe closed his notebook and stood, offering the housekeeper a sympathetic nod. "Thank you, Mrs. Cunningham. You've been very helpful."

As he left the room, Marlowe couldn't shake the feeling that the pieces were finally starting to come together. Charlotte had been trapped in a web of family pressures, secret deals, and hidden threats. Her relationship with her father had fractured under the weight of his expectations, and her brother, David, was entangled in something dangerous.

But who had made the final move? Who had silenced Charlotte before she could escape the life she had been born into?

Marlowe knew one thing for sure: the truth was buried in the twisted dynamics of the Winthrop family. And the closer he got to it, the more dangerous the game became.

Chapter 10: The Business Partner

Detective Jonathan Marlowe sat in a nondescript conference room downtown, the sterile fluorescent lights buzzing softly overhead. Across from him sat Richard Caldwell, a former business associate of the Winthrop family. Caldwell was a sharp-dressed man in his mid-50s, his salt-and-pepper hair slicked back with precision. His tailored suit and expensive watch told the story of a man who had tasted success, but the tightness around his eyes and the nervous tapping of his fingers on the table suggested someone who was no stranger to high-stakes games—games that often ended with people getting burned.

The Winthrops had built their wealth on real estate and development, but Marlowe had learned that the family's financial dealings were not as pristine as they appeared. Caldwell had been involved in some of those dealings—until he wasn't. His sudden departure from the Winthrop circle had raised eyebrows, and Marlowe had tracked him down to see if his falling-out with the family had anything to do with Charlotte's death.

"Thank you for agreeing to meet with me, Mr. Caldwell," Marlowe began, sitting back in his chair to observe the man carefully. "I understand you used to be involved with the Winthrop family's business ventures."

Caldwell nodded, though the wary look in his eyes remained. "That's right. For about ten years, I worked closely with William Winthrop. Real estate development, land acquisitions—mostly big projects. It was good business for a while."

"But then you parted ways," Marlowe pressed, leaning forward. "Why?"

Caldwell shifted in his seat, his gaze flickering away briefly before he met Marlowe's eyes again. "Let's just say things became... complicated. William and I had a difference of opinion on how certain business should be conducted. He's a man who likes control—total control—and I wasn't willing to go along with some of the deals he was making."

"What kind of deals?" Marlowe asked, his curiosity piqued.

Caldwell exhaled sharply, clearly reluctant to speak ill of the family, but something in his expression shifted—like he had been waiting for the opportunity to finally say his piece. "Shady deals. The Winthrop empire isn't built on just legitimate business practices, Detective. There were bribes, kickbacks, off-the-books transactions... you name it. And William had his hands in all of it."

Marlowe felt a cold knot tightening in his gut. He had expected the Winthrops to have some skeletons in their closet, but this went deeper than he'd imagined. "Was Charlotte involved in any of this?" he asked.

Caldwell hesitated, the flicker of discomfort returning. "Yes and no," he said finally. "She wasn't directly involved in the day-to-day operations, at least not when I was still working with them. But she knew about it. I think she was trying to distance herself from the family business—she wasn't like her father. She had her own ideas about how things should be run, and from what I've heard, that put her at odds with him."

Marlowe nodded. That fit with what he had already uncovered about the tension between Charlotte and her father. "Do you think she had plans to expose the corruption?"

Caldwell's eyes widened slightly, and he leaned back in his chair, considering the question. "It's possible," he said slowly. "She was smart—smarter than people gave her credit for. I always got the sense she wasn't happy with how things were being handled. She may have been biding her time, waiting for the right moment to make a move. But if she had any intention of going public with what she knew, it would have been dangerous. William Winthrop doesn't take kindly to betrayal."

Marlowe scribbled notes, his mind racing with possibilities. "Did she have anyone in particular she might have confided in? Someone who could have helped her if she wanted to blow the whistle?"

Caldwell shook his head. "I don't know. Charlotte kept her personal life private. I didn't have much contact with her directly after I left the company. But if she was planning to expose her father's dealings, she would have needed leverage—proof. Without it, her accusations wouldn't stand a chance."

"Proof," Marlowe repeated, thinking of Charlotte's secretive behaviour in the months leading up to her death. Could she have been gathering evidence? If so, where was it now?

He switched gears slightly. "You said earlier that your relationship with the family ended over a disagreement about business practices. Was there a specific deal that caused the fallout?"

Caldwell's expression darkened. "Yeah. There was a development project about three years ago—prime real estate, but the deal involved underhanded tactics to force people off their land. I couldn't stomach it. William, on the other hand, was willing to do whatever it took to secure the deal, even if it meant ruining lives."

"Did Charlotte know about this particular deal?" Marlowe asked, his mind churning.

Caldwell nodded. "She knew. I heard from some mutual contacts that she confronted her father about it. She told him she didn't want to be associated with a company that did things like that. I think that's when the real tension between them started. She was pushing for the company to clean up its act, but William wasn't interested. He had too much at stake."

Marlowe leaned back, the pieces falling into place. "And you believe that tension was still ongoing?"

"Absolutely," Caldwell replied. "Charlotte was strong-willed, but she was up against her father, who had spent his entire life building that empire. She didn't stand a chance unless she had something concrete to use against him."

Marlowe paused, considering everything Caldwell had told him. Charlotte had known about the corruption in her family's business, and she had been deeply troubled by it. She had clashed with her father over it, and it was possible she had been gathering evidence to expose him. But someone had silenced her before she could act.

"One more thing," Marlowe said. "Were there any other players involved in these shady deals—anyone who might have had a vested interest in keeping Charlotte quiet?"

Caldwell's face hardened. "A lot of people were involved in those deals, Detective. Developers, investors, even politicians. If Charlotte was planning to expose her father's dirty laundry, it wouldn't just have been William who wanted to stop her. There are people out there who would do anything to protect their interests."

Marlowe's stomach tightened. The web of corruption was far more tangled than he had initially thought. It wasn't just a family drama—it was a dangerous game with high stakes, and Charlotte had been caught in the middle.

"Thank you for your time, Mr. Caldwell," Marlowe said, standing up. "You've given me a lot to think about."

Caldwell stood as well, his expression grim. "Be careful, Detective. The Winthrops aren't the only ones who have secrets to protect. If you dig too deep, you might not like what you find."

Marlowe nodded, the warning echoing in his mind as he left the room. As he walked back toward the station, the weight of the case settled heavily on his shoulders.

Charlotte Winthrop had been trying to escape her family's legacy of greed and corruption. But in doing so, she had made enemies—dangerous enemies.

And one of them had ensured she never got the chance to break free.

Chapter 11: The Heirloom Necklace

The rain tapped softly against the tall windows of the Winthrop mansion as Detective Marlowe stood in Charlotte's bedroom once again, the air heavy with the scent of damp earth and decay. He had been here before—meticulously combing through the pristine facade of the heiress's personal life. But this time, something felt different. After interviewing Richard Caldwell and learning about the web of corruption entangling the family, Marlowe was certain there was more to Charlotte's death than just family tension.

Marlowe's eyes drifted to the dresser, where a velvet-lined jewellery box sat, partially open. When he had first examined Charlotte's belongings, the box had seemed innocuous—filled with the kind of priceless heirlooms you'd expect from a family like the Winthrops. But something had caught his attention during his most recent interview with Eleanor Winthrop, Charlotte's mother.

She had spoken in a soft, broken voice, recounting the family's most treasured heirloom: a diamond and sapphire necklace that had been passed down from generation to generation, always worn by the women of the Winthrop line at special family events. Eleanor had assumed Charlotte would be the next in line to wear it, but when Marlowe asked about it, her face paled.

"It's missing," she had whispered, her voice barely audible. "I... I hadn't thought about it until now. Charlotte was supposed to wear it at the charity gala a few months ago, but she refused. I haven't seen it since."

Now, standing in Charlotte's room, Marlowe's eyes narrowed as he examined the contents of the jewellery box again. It was filled with various pieces of expensive jewellery—pearls, gold bracelets, and diamond rings—but there was no sign of the heirloom necklace.

He lifted the velvet tray, revealing the compartment beneath, hoping the necklace might have been tucked away. But the space was empty.

Marlowe's mind raced. The necklace's disappearance wasn't just an oversight. Charlotte had refused to wear it at the gala, and now it was missing entirely. A priceless family heirloom like that didn't just vanish without someone noticing.

He turned to Suarez, who had been helping him search the room. "The necklace isn't here," he said quietly. "The one Eleanor mentioned—the diamond and sapphire piece. It's gone."

Suarez looked up from the stack of papers she had been sifting through, her brow furrowing. "That's odd. You'd think someone in the family would have noticed."

"Eleanor did," Marlowe replied, "but she assumed Charlotte had it. Apparently, Charlotte refused to wear it to an event recently, which seems out of character given how important it is to the family."

Suarez crossed her arms, leaning against the dresser. "So what does that mean? She hid it? Gave it to someone?"

Marlowe considered the possibilities. "If she didn't want to wear it, there's a chance it symbolized something more to her. Maybe she was rejecting the family's legacy—or maybe there's a more practical reason it's gone. What if someone took it?"

"A theft?" Suarez asked, her eyes narrowing. "If the necklace is worth as much as we think, that could be motive enough. But who would have access to it?"

"That's the question," Marlowe muttered. "The family claims it's been missing for months. No one seems to know exactly when it disappeared."

Suarez thought for a moment. "It could have been taken around the same time that Charlotte started to distance herself from the family business. Maybe someone saw an opportunity and took it. But why hasn't it been reported? Surely, if something that valuable was stolen, the family would have notified the police."

Marlowe shook his head. "Not necessarily. The Winthrops are the type to handle things quietly. If the necklace had gone missing and someone inside the family was involved, they'd do everything they could to avoid a scandal."

Suarez frowned. "So you think someone in the family took it?"

"It's possible," Marlowe said, pacing the room. "But it could also be someone from the outside. A lover, a business associate... someone who had access to Charlotte and her things."

Suarez flipped through her notebook, where she had been keeping track of everything they'd uncovered so far. "What about Mark Hayes? He admitted to being in a relationship with Charlotte, and we know he was close to her in the months leading up to her death."

Marlowe paused, considering the possibility. Mark hadn't seemed like the type to be after Charlotte's wealth—his feelings for her had appeared genuine—but Marlowe had learned not to take anything at face value.

"It's worth following up on," Marlowe agreed. "But if Hayes didn't take the necklace, someone else did. And whoever has it now might know more than they're letting on."

Later that day, Marlowe and Suarez met with Mark Hayes at a small café downtown. Mark looked weary, the strain of Charlotte's death still heavy on his face, but he had agreed to meet with them again to answer more questions.

"Mark, I need to ask you something about Charlotte," Marlowe began after they exchanged brief pleasantries. "Her family had a priceless heirloom—an old diamond and sapphire necklace. Have you ever seen it?"

Mark frowned, clearly confused. "I don't think so. Charlotte didn't really care about that kind of stuff. She was always talking about how the family's wealth was more of a burden than a blessing."

Marlowe nodded. "Did she ever mention the necklace to you? Refuse to wear it, or give you any indication that it was important to the family?"

Mark shook his head. "No. She hated being paraded around at their charity events and galas, but she never mentioned any necklace."

Marlowe studied Mark's expression, searching for any hint of deception, but found none. If Mark knew about the necklace, he wasn't letting on. "Do you know if Charlotte gave any of her belongings to someone? A gift, perhaps? Something valuable?"

Mark's face tightened, and for a moment, Marlowe thought he saw a flicker of realization cross his face. "Actually... she did give me something. Not jewellery, but a box of documents."

"Documents?" Marlowe asked, his interest piqued.

Mark nodded. "Yeah. A couple of weeks before she died, she showed up at my apartment with this old wooden box. She said it was important and asked me to keep it safe for her. I didn't open it—she made me promise not to—but she looked scared, like whatever was inside could get her in trouble."

Marlowe exchanged a quick glance with Suarez. "Do you still have the box?"

"Yeah," Mark said. "It's at my apartment. I haven't touched it since she gave it to me."

Marlowe leaned forward, his heart pounding. "Mark, I need to see that box. It could be the key to understanding what was really going on with Charlotte."

Later that evening, Marlowe and Suarez stood in Mark's apartment as he pulled the wooden box from the back of a closet. It was an old, ornate box, its hinges creaking as Mark carefully opened the lid.

Inside were papers—contracts, letters, financial documents, and... at the very bottom, nestled beneath the stack of papers, was a velvet pouch.

Marlowe's breath caught as he reached inside and pulled it out. He opened the pouch, revealing the unmistakable gleam of diamonds and sapphires. The missing heirloom necklace.

"This is it," Marlowe whispered. "The necklace."

Mark looked stunned. "I had no idea it was in there."

Marlowe examined the necklace closely. It wasn't just a symbol of the Winthrop family's legacy—it was a clue, hidden in plain sight. Charlotte had been keeping it away from her family, but why? And what did the documents in the box have to do with it?

As Marlowe and Suarez sifted through the papers, the full scope of the conspiracy surrounding Charlotte's death began to take shape.

The missing necklace had been more than just a valuable piece of jewellery. It was a symbol of rebellion, of secrets Charlotte had been trying to protect—and it had cost her everything.

Chapter 12: The Estranged Aunt

The small town of Whitefield was a world away from the opulence of the Winthrop estate. Tucked into a quiet corner of the countryside, it was the kind of place where life moved slowly, and the past had a way of lingering in the air. It was here, in a modest cottage on the outskirts of town, that Detective Jonathan Marlowe found Vivian Winthrop, the long-estranged sister of William Winthrop.

Vivian had been exiled from the family decades ago, her name rarely spoken within the Winthrop household. The details of her departure had always been murky, but Marlowe had uncovered a reference to her during his investigation. She had once been a significant figure in the family's inner circle—until something drove a wedge between her and her brother. If anyone knew the dark history behind the Winthrop legacy, it would be her.

As Marlowe approached the door, he was struck by the simplicity of the place. The cottage was small, its garden overgrown with wildflowers and ivy creeping up the stone walls. It was a stark contrast to the grandeur of the Winthrop estate, but it had a certain charm, a peacefulness that was absent from the mansion's suffocating halls.

Vivian answered the door after a few moments, her sharp blue eyes narrowing as she took in the detective standing before her. She was older than he had expected—her grey hair pulled into a loose bun, and her posture slightly hunched from years of hard living—but there was a fierce intelligence behind her gaze. She looked as though she had seen too much and survived it all.

"You must be the detective," she said, her voice raspy but strong. "I wondered when someone would come looking for me."

Marlowe nodded. "Vivian Winthrop, I presume?"

She smiled thinly. "That's right, though I haven't gone by that name in a long time. Come in, Detective. I suppose you're here to dig up some old bones."

Marlowe stepped inside the cozy but cluttered living room, the smell of wood smoke lingering in the air. Vivian gestured for him to sit in an old armchair while she settled into the chair across from him.

"I appreciate you agreeing to speak with me," Marlowe began, taking out his notebook. "I'm investigating the death of your niece, Charlotte Winthrop."

Vivian's eyes flickered with recognition, but there was no surprise in her expression. "Poor Charlotte. I always knew she was trapped in that house, just like the rest of us were. But I suppose you're here to ask about the family's dirty laundry, aren't you?"

Marlowe didn't hesitate. "I've heard that there was tension in the family—particularly when it came to matters of inheritance and control. I was hoping you could shed some light on that."

Vivian let out a dry, humourless laugh. "Tension? That's putting it mildly. The Winthrop family has always been divided, Detective. Money and power do that to people. It's been that way for generations. William and I were no different."

"What happened between you and your brother?" Marlowe asked, sensing that the answer might explain more than just a sibling rivalry.

Vivian's gaze hardened, and she folded her hands in her lap, the knuckles white with tension. "William and I were close once—when we were younger. We were raised to believe that the family legacy was everything. But when our father died, things changed. William took control of the family business, and I... well, I was left with nothing. I didn't want the business. I wanted my freedom, but William saw that as a betrayal."

"Why did he see it that way?" Marlowe pressed.

"Because to William, the family legacy is everything," Vivian said bitterly. "He believed that I was turning my back on our father's empire, on the life we were supposed to uphold. But I couldn't live like that, under the weight of those expectations. We fought—over the business, over our inheritance, over control. And eventually, William cut me off completely."

Marlowe frowned. "He cut you off? From the family estate?"

Vivian nodded, her expression cold. "Yes. I was written out of the will, disinherited. It was his way of punishing me for leaving, for daring to live my life outside the confines of the Winthrop empire."

Marlowe absorbed the information, the picture of William Winthrop becoming clearer. A man obsessed with control, with preserving the family's wealth and legacy at any cost. It was easy to see how Charlotte, raised under the same expectations, might have felt similarly trapped.

"Was Charlotte aware of this history?" Marlowe asked.

Vivian's eyes softened, and for the first time, Marlowe saw a hint of sorrow in her expression. "I believe she was. We spoke once, a few years ago, before things got really bad between her and William. She came to see me—curious, I think, about why I had left the family. I told her the truth, about how our father's death had torn the family apart. She was struggling, even then, with the weight of what was expected of her."

Marlowe leaned forward, his curiosity deepening. "And what did she say?"

"She said she felt like she was living someone else's life," Vivian replied quietly. "Like she was just another cog in the machine her father had built. She wanted to escape, to live on her own terms. But she didn't know how."

Marlowe's thoughts returned to the missing necklace and the box of documents Mark Hayes had mentioned. Charlotte had been gathering leverage—possibly to free herself from her father's control. "Vivian, do you know if Charlotte was planning anything? Something that might have threatened William's control over the family's wealth?"

Vivian's expression darkened. "If she was, it wouldn't surprise me. William never tolerated dissent—especially from his own children. He wanted them under his thumb, just like he wanted me. But Charlotte was different. She had a fire in her, a desire to break free."

Marlowe nodded slowly. "Did you ever hear anything about the family's heirloom necklace? The one that's missing?"

Vivian's face tightened. "The necklace... yes, I remember that cursed thing. It's been passed down for generations, a symbol of the family's power. My mother wore it, and so did I—until I was exiled. I always thought of it as a chain, binding us to the family's legacy. If Charlotte refused to wear it, I wouldn't blame her."

Marlowe absorbed the weight of her words. The necklace wasn't just a piece of jewellery—it was a symbol of the expectations and control that had suffocated Charlotte, just as it had suffocated Vivian before her.

"Vivian," Marlowe said, his voice calm but firm, "do you think someone in the family could have killed Charlotte to protect the family's legacy?"

Vivian was silent for a long moment, her gaze distant. Then she looked directly at Marlowe, her eyes filled with a sadness that ran deep. "I wouldn't put it past them, Detective. William would do anything to keep his empire intact. If Charlotte was a threat... well, the Winthrops have always been willing to sacrifice their own to protect what they've built."

Marlowe felt a chill crawl down his spine. The tangled web of family loyalty, betrayal, and greed had deep roots, stretching back generations. And now, those same forces had cost Charlotte her life.

"Thank you, Vivian," Marlowe said quietly, standing to leave. "You've been very helpful."

Vivian gave a sad, knowing smile. "Be careful, Detective. You're dealing with people who value power above all else. And in this family, power has a way of destroying everything it touches."

As Marlowe left the cottage, the weight of what he had learned pressed heavily on his shoulders. The Winthrop family was more than just a wealthy dynasty—it was a legacy built on control, on the sacrifice of those who dared to defy it. And now, it had claimed another victim.

Charlotte had tried to break free from her family's grip. But in doing so, she had ignited a fire that had consumed her—and perhaps others were willing to ensure that it never spread further.

Marlowe knew one thing for certain: the Winthrop legacy was rotten to its core, and the deeper he dug, the more dangerous the truth became.

Chapter 13: The Will

The grand sitting room of the Winthrop estate was uncomfortably silent. The tension was palpable, hanging in the air like a storm about to break. The family members sat around the long, polished mahogany table, their expressions tense and unreadable. William Winthrop sat at the head of the table, his cold gaze fixed on the far wall, his hands clasped tightly in front of him. Eleanor, pale and trembling, sat to his right, her eyes downcast, clutching a handkerchief. David, restless and fidgety, sat opposite his father, his eyes darting nervously around the room.

In the center of it all, Henry Lawson, the family lawyer, sat with a leather briefcase on the table before him. He cleared his throat, adjusting his glasses as he opened the briefcase and pulled out a thick envelope—the will of Charlotte Winthrop.

Marlowe and Suarez stood quietly by the doorway, observing the scene with sharp eyes. The reading of the will had the potential to unearth long-buried tensions, and Marlowe knew that the truth behind Charlotte's death might finally begin to surface here, in this room.

"Thank you all for gathering today," Henry Lawson began, his voice formal and businesslike. "As you know, the purpose of this meeting is to read the last will and testament of Charlotte Winthrop."

He paused, unfolding the document and smoothing it out on the table. The tension in the room thickened as everyone waited, the anticipation almost unbearable.

Lawson began to read: "I, Charlotte Annabelle Winthrop, being of sound mind and body, do hereby declare this to be my last will and testament. To my mother, Eleanor Winthrop, I leave the entirety of my personal jewellery collection, including the pieces passed down through the family."

Eleanor sniffed softly, dabbing her eyes, but said nothing.

"To my brother, David Winthrop," Lawson continued, "I leave my personal estate in Whitefield, including the cottage and surrounding lands, to be used as he sees fit."

David blinked in surprise but didn't say anything. The cottage was valuable, but it wasn't the inheritance he had been expecting.

Lawson hesitated for a moment, glancing briefly at William before he continued reading. "To my father, William Winthrop, I leave... nothing."

A sharp, audible intake of breath rippled through the room.

William's eyes flashed with fury, but he remained silent, his jaw clenched so tightly Marlowe thought it might shatter. The room was frozen, the weight of Charlotte's decision hanging in the air like a blade.

Lawson cleared his throat awkwardly and continued, "The bulk of my estate, including my shares in the Winthrop family business, my financial assets, and any remaining property, will be placed into a charitable foundation to be established in my name. The foundation's mission will be to support women seeking independence from oppressive family structures, to promote education, and to provide assistance to those in need."

A stunned silence followed the announcement, broken only by the sound of Eleanor's soft sobbing. William's face was a mask of cold fury, and David sat back in his chair, wide-eyed, his expression a mix of confusion and shock.

Marlowe watched the family's reactions carefully. Charlotte's will had upended their expectations. The family wealth, the empire that William had built, was now largely out of their hands. Charlotte's decision to disinherit her father and create a foundation dedicated to helping women escape oppressive families spoke volumes about her state of mind before her death. She had been trying to break free from the grip of her father's control—and she had chosen to leave a legacy that would do the same for others.

Henry Lawson closed the will and folded his hands on the table. "That concludes the reading of the will. The details of the charitable foundation will be handled in due course, but this document is legally binding and has been properly executed."

The room was still. William's icy silence spoke louder than any outburst. His daughter, the one he had groomed to continue the family legacy, had not only rejected that role—she had effectively dismantled his control over her wealth and the family business.

David broke the silence first, his voice low and trembling. "She left me the cottage? And the rest—she just gave it away? To charity?"

Lawson nodded solemnly. "That's correct. The foundation will manage her assets going forward. David, you are entitled to the cottage and the land surrounding it, as specified."

David looked around the room, bewildered. He seemed almost at a loss for words. "I don't understand," he muttered. "Why would she do this? Why would she cut out Father?"

William's voice, cold and hard as steel, finally broke through the air. "She was weak," he spat, his tone venomous. "She never understood the importance of the family's legacy. She was too soft—too easily manipulated by outside influences. And now, this... this charity?" He practically hissed the word. "She's given away everything I worked for. She was a fool."

Eleanor flinched at his words but said nothing, her grief-stricken eyes fixed on the table.

Marlowe exchanged a glance with Suarez. The will had revealed more than just the distribution of Charlotte's assets—it had exposed the fractures in the family that had led to her death. Charlotte had been planning to sever ties with her father's empire, and her decision to create a foundation that directly opposed the values of the Winthrop family showed just how deeply she had resented the life she had been forced to lead.

But more importantly, the contents of the will had created new motives. William, stripped of his daughter's wealth and the control he had sought to maintain, now had every reason to want her out of the picture. The will wasn't just an inheritance—it was an act of defiance, and William's reaction was telling.

Marlowe turned to Henry Lawson. "Was anyone aware of the contents of Charlotte's will before today?"

Lawson shook his head. "No. Charlotte made these changes several months ago, shortly after a major argument with her father. She was very clear about her wishes, but she wanted everything kept private until the time came."

"And no one in the family knew?" Suarez pressed.

"Correct," Lawson replied. "She kept the details of the will between us and her legal advisors."

Marlowe nodded, understanding the weight of that decision. Charlotte had been careful—careful enough to hide her true intentions until it was too late for anyone to interfere. But someone might have suspected. And someone might have acted to ensure that Charlotte never lived to see her plans come to fruition.

As Marlowe and Suarez prepared to leave the estate, the tension in the room was still thick. William sat rigidly in his chair, his face a mask of cold fury, while David stared blankly at the will in front of him, still trying to process the shock.

The reading of the will had revealed more than just the distribution of wealth. It had exposed the deep fractures in the Winthrop family, the resentments, and the motivations that had driven them all. Charlotte's decision to sever her ties with her father's empire had set off a chain reaction—one that might have led to her death.

As Marlowe stepped out into the cold air, he knew that the investigation had just entered a new, dangerous phase. The will had changed everything. And now, it was time to confront the person who had the most to lose.

Chapter 14: The Lake's Curse

The wind whistled through the towering pines that lined the shores of the Winthrop family's private lake, its surface still and dark like a sheet of polished obsidian. Detective Marlowe stood at the water's edge, gazing out over the ominous expanse, his mind weighed down by the unsettling tales he had heard in town. The locals called it "the cursed lake." For generations, it had been the site of mysterious accidents, disappearances, and tragedies—each one deepening the myth that the lake was somehow... cursed.

He had come here not just to ponder the growing pile of evidence in Charlotte's death, but to explore the disturbing stories that had swirled around this lake for as long as anyone could remember. The Winthrop family had always been the center of power and wealth in this part of the world, but the lake was something else—something the family, and the town itself, couldn't quite control.

Earlier that day, Marlowe had spent hours interviewing townspeople at the local diner. He had intended to gather more mundane information—any rumours or leads that might help his case—but instead, he was met with tales of shadows in the water, mysterious drownings, and a persistent belief that the lake held dark, unnatural powers.

"That lake's got a way of keeping secrets," one elderly woman had said, shaking her head. "You don't go swimming there at night. And you sure as hell don't go near it if you've got a guilty conscience. That's why the Winthrops don't talk about it much."

Another man, a fisherman, had chimed in. "There've been at least three drownings that I know of, and none of 'em made sense. No storms, no accidents. People just vanish into that water. It's like it's alive, waiting for someone to slip up."

The stories had been a mix of folklore and fact, superstition and half-remembered incidents, but they all seemed to have one thing in common—the lake had a reputation for taking lives, especially those connected to the Winthrop family.

Marlowe glanced down at his notebook, where he had scribbled some of the key details. There had been strange accidents stretching back decades, but two stood out to him as eerily similar to Charlotte's death.

In the 1920s, a Winthrop ancestor named Margaret Winthrop had drowned in the lake under mysterious circumstances. According to local legend, she had been seen walking along the shore late one night, arguing with her husband. The next morning, her body was found floating in the exact spot where Charlotte's had been discovered nearly a century later. Her death had been ruled an accident, but the town had whispered for years that it was no accident—that something in the lake had pulled her under.

Then, in the 1960s, a child from a neighbouring estate had disappeared while playing near the lake. His body was never found, though locals claimed they had heard cries for help coming from the water that night, only to find nothing when they searched. That incident, too, had been buried, attributed to the mischief of a young boy straying too far from home.

Now, with Charlotte's death, the lake had claimed yet another life, and the old stories were stirring again.

As Marlowe stood there, the chill in the air seemed to deepen, the temperature dropping noticeably as the wind picked up. He couldn't help but feel a strange sense of unease as he stared into the black water, the surface so smooth it reflected the sky like a mirror. It was almost as if the lake was watching him, waiting for him to make the next move.

"Detective Marlowe."

The sudden voice behind him startled him from his thoughts. He turned to see Sam Pritchard, the local groundskeeper who had worked on the Winthrop estate for as long as anyone could remember.

Pritchard was an older man, his weathered face deeply lined from years spent outdoors, and his eyes held a kind of hard-won wisdom.

"I didn't mean to scare you," Pritchard said, his voice rough but friendly. "Figured you might want to hear a thing or two about this lake. It's not just the town that talks."

Marlowe gave a nod of acknowledgment. "I've been hearing plenty of stories. People seem to think this place has a mind of its own."

Pritchard's expression darkened as he approached, his boots crunching on the gravelly shore. "I've worked here long enough to know better than to dismiss those stories outright. I've seen things, heard things that'll make the hair on your neck stand up."

"What kind of things?" Marlowe asked, intrigued. Pritchard had been working here for decades, and if anyone knew the hidden history of the lake, it would be him.

Pritchard glanced out over the water, his eyes narrowing. "Strange lights, ripples when there's no wind. On some nights, you can hear voices out here. Not real voices—like echoes, coming from the lake itself. And people who don't belong here... well, the lake don't take kindly to them."

Marlowe raised an eyebrow. "You think the lake has something to do with Charlotte's death?"

Pritchard shrugged, but his face remained grim. "I don't know what happened to Miss Charlotte, but I know that lake has a way of keeping secrets. If she was mixed up in something, maybe the lake helped settle the score. Or maybe someone used the lake's reputation to cover their tracks."

That last comment struck Marlowe. The stories, the legends, the superstitions—they were all swirling together, creating a perfect veil for anyone who wanted to hide a crime. After all, who would question a drowning in a place with such a dark history?

"Do you think someone would use these old legends to hide what really happened?" Marlowe asked, probing for more.

Pritchard nodded slowly. "It's possible. There's plenty of folks who believe in the curse, but there's also those who know how to use it to their advantage. If someone wanted Charlotte dead, they could make it look like the lake took her—like it's done before."

Marlowe felt a chill run down his spine, though it wasn't from the cold. The idea that someone might have exploited the lake's dark reputation to stage Charlotte's death made a disturbing amount of sense. It would explain why her drowning had seemed so clean, so carefully orchestrated. But it didn't explain why.

"Was there anyone in particular who was interested in the lake recently?" Marlowe asked. "Anyone who might have been poking around or asking questions?"

Pritchard scratched his chin thoughtfully. "Now that you mention it, there was a visitor a few weeks back. Some guy—real estate type, I think. He was asking about the lake, about the land surrounding it. Said he was interested in buying it."

Marlowe's ears perked up. "Did he leave a name?"

Pritchard shook his head. "Didn't catch it. But he didn't stick around long. Just asked a few questions, then left. I didn't think much of it at the time."

Marlowe's mind raced. Could this visitor have been involved in Charlotte's death? Had she stumbled upon something—some deal or hidden agenda—that had put her life in danger?

As the sun dipped lower on the horizon, casting long shadows across the lake, Marlowe turned back to Pritchard. "If you think of anything else, anything that might help, let me know."

Pritchard gave a curt nod. "I'll keep my ears open."

As Marlowe walked away from the lake, the wind at his back, he couldn't shake the feeling that the answers he sought lay beneath the water's dark surface. The legends surrounding the lake were more than just ghost stories—they were part of the tangled web of mystery surrounding the Winthrop family.

The lake had kept its secrets for generations. But Marlowe was determined to uncover the truth—no matter how deep it was buried.

Chapter 15: A Childhood Friend

The small café in Whitefield had the charm of a place that had seen countless conversations over the years—some full of laughter, others tinged with sadness. Today, it would bear witness to another difficult discussion. Detective Jonathan Marlowe sat at a corner table, waiting for Isabelle Dawes, Charlotte Winthrop's childhood friend. Marlowe had tracked her down after hearing murmurs in town about her past closeness with Charlotte. The two had grown up together, spending summers at the Winthrop estate, but their friendship had quietly faded as they got older.

Still, Isabelle was one of the few people who had known Charlotte before the pressures of family legacy had begun to suffocate her. Marlowe hoped she could shed light on the girl Charlotte had once been—and perhaps, reveal secrets about the woman she had become.

The bell above the door jingled, and Marlowe looked up to see Isabelle enter. She was in her early thirties, with soft brown hair that framed a face marked by concern and curiosity. She wore a simple coat, her hands tucked into the pockets, and her eyes scanned the room before meeting Marlowe's. She approached with a cautious smile.

"Detective Marlowe?" she asked.

He stood and offered his hand. "Ms. Dawes, thank you for meeting with me."

"Isabelle, please," she replied, shaking his hand and taking a seat across from him. "It's strange being back here. I haven't thought about the Winthrops in years, but hearing about Charlotte... I just—well, I can't believe it."

Marlowe nodded, sensing the emotion in her voice. "I'm sorry for your loss. I know this must be difficult. Charlotte's death has raised many questions, and I was hoping you could help me understand more about her—about the Charlotte you knew."

Isabelle sighed softly, running a hand through her hair as she thought. "It's been a long time, Detective. We were so close as children. Summers at the estate were like a dream back then. But as we got older, things changed. Charlotte changed."

Marlowe leaned forward, listening intently. "What changed? Was it something specific?"

Isabelle hesitated, her eyes distant, as if she were looking back through years of memories. "It wasn't just one thing. The Winthrops have always been... intense. The weight of their family's name, their wealth—it shaped everything. As kids, we were sheltered from most of it, but I could always sense that Charlotte was under a lot of pressure. Her father, William, was strict. He expected perfection. Charlotte felt that burden more than anyone."

Marlowe nodded. "Did she talk to you about it?"

"Not at first," Isabelle replied, her voice growing quieter. "But as we got older, things began to change. When we were about twelve or thirteen, there was a shift in Charlotte. She became more withdrawn, more anxious about the future. She would tell me things—things that frightened her."

"Frightened her?" Marlowe asked, his interest piqued. "What kinds of things?"

Isabelle paused, biting her lip. "There was one incident... something I've never told anyone about. We were thirteen, I think, and it was late summer. We had been playing down by the lake, like we always did, but that day, something was different. Charlotte had been quiet all afternoon, and when I asked her what was wrong, she told me she'd had a terrible dream the night before."

Marlowe raised an eyebrow. "A dream?"

Isabelle nodded, her voice trembling slightly. "She said in the dream, she was standing by the lake at night, alone. The water was dark, but she could see something—or someone—moving beneath the surface. She told me she felt this overwhelming sense of dread, like something was watching her, waiting to pull her under. And then, in the dream, she stepped closer to the edge of the lake, and the water reached out for her, pulling her in."

Marlowe felt a chill run down his spine. "And that was just a dream?"

"At first, yes," Isabelle continued. "But after that, she refused to go near the lake at night. She was terrified of it. And the weird thing is, strange things started happening after that. One evening, we were sitting near the shore, watching the sunset, when Charlotte suddenly stood up and said she had to go back to the house. She was pale, shaking, like she had seen something. When I asked her what was wrong, she just said, 'It's not safe here anymore.'"

Marlowe frowned, scribbling notes in his notebook. "Did she ever explain what she meant?"

"No," Isabelle said, her voice growing quieter. "But after that summer, everything changed. Charlotte started pulling away from me, from everyone. She became more serious, more reserved. And she started spending more time with her father—learning about the family business, attending all those formal events. It was like she was preparing for something."

"Did you ever talk to her about what was happening?" Marlowe asked.

"I tried," Isabelle replied, her face clouded with regret. "But every time I brought it up, she would shut down. Eventually, we just... drifted apart. I went to boarding school, and Charlotte stayed at the estate. I'd hear things through mutual friends—how she was being groomed to take over the family business, how the pressure was getting to her—but we never reconnected."

Marlowe leaned back, considering everything Isabelle had told him. The dream by the lake, Charlotte's growing anxiety, her sudden withdrawal from friends—it all painted a picture of a girl haunted by something, long before the pressures of the family business had fully taken hold. And now, with Charlotte's death occurring in the same lake that had filled her childhood with dread, it felt like an eerie premonition fulfilled.

"Isabelle," Marlowe said carefully, "do you think Charlotte was afraid of her father? Or the expectations he placed on her?"

Isabelle hesitated for a moment, then nodded. "Yes. I do. William was always controlling, always demanding perfection. Charlotte was the heir to everything—she couldn't escape it. And I think... deep down, she knew that no matter how hard she tried, she would never be free."

Marlowe's mind raced. The lake had always been a symbol of fear for Charlotte, and now it had become her final resting place. But was it more than just a tragic coincidence? Had Charlotte's deep-seated fear of the lake, of her family's legacy, somehow played a role in her death?

"Did Charlotte ever talk about wanting to leave?" Marlowe asked. "To escape her family?"

Isabelle's eyes filled with sadness. "She mentioned it once, years ago, when we were still close. She said that one day, she would find a way to get out—to live her life on her own terms. But I think she knew, even then, that it was just a fantasy."

Marlowe nodded, absorbing the weight of Isabelle's words. Charlotte had been trapped in more ways than one—by her family, by her responsibilities, and perhaps even by her own fears. The lake had always loomed large in her life, both as a place of childhood play and as a source of inexplicable terror. And now, it had claimed her.

"Thank you, Isabelle," Marlowe said, standing. "You've been very helpful."

As Marlowe left the café, the pieces of the puzzle began to shift in his mind. Charlotte's death was no accident—it was the culmination of years of fear, control, and hidden trauma. But there was still one crucial question left to answer: Who had made the final, fatal move?

The lake held its secrets, and so did the Winthrop family. But now, Marlowe was closer than ever to uncovering the truth—one that had been buried deep, beneath years of lies and darkness.

Chapter 16: The Boatman's Story

The scent of wet pine and the sharp chill of early evening clung to the air as Detective Jonathan Marlowe approached the small wooden boathouse at the edge of the Winthrop family lake. The structure, worn with age and weather, creaked softly in the breeze, its door slightly ajar as if inviting him in. Inside, Tom Granger, the boatman who had worked the lake for years, sat on an overturned crate, a cigarette hanging loosely from his lips.

Granger was a local fixture, a man who knew the lake better than most—better, perhaps, than anyone. His weathered face, leathery from years in the sun, gave him the look of someone who had seen too much. The townspeople had spoken of him with mixed emotions: some thought him odd but harmless, while others believed he knew more about the lake's dark history than he let on.

Marlowe had tracked Granger down after hearing that he might have been near the lake on the night of Charlotte Winthrop's death. But something about the way Granger had avoided the authorities until now suggested he wasn't eager to talk. Marlowe intended to change that.

"Tom Granger?" Marlowe asked as he stepped into the dim light of the boathouse.

Granger looked up, his faded blue eyes narrowing slightly. "That's me," he said, his voice a raspy drawl. He took a long drag from his cigarette before stubbing it out on the crate. "You're the detective, aren't you? Come to ask about the lake, I reckon."

Marlowe nodded, stepping closer. "That's right. I'm investigating Charlotte Winthrop's death, and I've heard you might have been near the lake that night."

Granger's eyes flickered, and he shifted uncomfortably, but he gave a slow nod. "I was there, yeah. I usually keep to myself, but sometimes I go out on the water late at night. Calms my mind, you know?"

Marlowe crossed his arms, watching the older man closely. "You were out there the night Charlotte died?"

Granger hesitated, glancing down at the floor. "I was," he admitted, his voice low. "Didn't think much of it at the time, but... yeah, I saw something."

Marlowe felt a flicker of anticipation. This could be the break he'd been looking for. "What did you see?"

Granger rubbed his chin, stalling for a moment. "Well, it was late. Must've been close to midnight. I was out in the boat, just drifting along the edge of the lake when I saw movement near the shore. At first, I thought it was an animal, but then I saw it was a person. A woman. She was standing real close to the water, just staring out at it."

Marlowe's mind raced. "Was it Charlotte?"

Granger nodded slowly. "Pretty sure it was. I'd seen her around before, out by the lake sometimes, but this was different. She looked... off. Like something was bothering her. She was pacing back and forth, looking out over the water like she was waiting for something. Or someone."

Marlowe's brow furrowed. "And you're sure it was Charlotte?"

Granger shrugged. "I'm not a hundred percent, but it sure looked like her. That fancy nightgown she always wore, her hair loose like she'd been out there for a while."

Marlowe felt a surge of curiosity. "Did you see anyone else? Was there anyone else on the shore or near the lake?"

Granger shifted in his seat, his eyes darting away for a brief moment before he answered. "Not at first. But after a while, I thought I saw something in the trees behind her. Just a shadow, maybe. Could've been nothing, but it made me uneasy. I turned the boat around and drifted farther out into the lake, didn't want to get involved."

Marlowe leaned forward, his voice sharpening. "A shadow? You didn't get a better look? Did anyone approach her?"

Granger's eyes flickered with uncertainty, and he shook his head. "I couldn't see clearly. The moon was out, but the trees cast long shadows. Could've been someone, could've been my imagination. But I'll tell you this—after a few minutes, Charlotte walked right to the edge of the lake and just stood there. Didn't move, didn't call out. It was like she was in a trance or something."

Marlowe frowned. "And then what happened?"

Granger swallowed, his voice barely above a whisper now. "I don't know. I turned my back for a minute, maybe less, and when I looked again, she was gone. Just... gone. I didn't hear a splash or anything. One minute she was there, the next she wasn't."

Marlowe's pulse quickened. "Gone? You mean she disappeared into the water?"

Granger nodded slowly, his face pale. "I didn't want to get any closer after that. I rowed back to the boathouse, and I've been trying not to think about it since."

Marlowe stared at Granger, his mind racing. The old man's story had a strange, unsettling quality to it—almost as if he were holding something back. The pacing, the trance-like state, the shadow in the trees—it all painted a picture of a woman who wasn't herself that night. But something about Granger's evasiveness suggested that there was more to his story.

"Tom," Marlowe said, his voice firm but calm, "you saw more than you're telling me. What else happened out there?"

Granger's hands began to tremble slightly, and he reached for another cigarette, lighting it with shaking fingers. He took a long drag before exhaling slowly. "I... I don't know what you mean, Detective."

Marlowe didn't let up. "You said there was a shadow in the trees. You think someone was there, don't you? Someone who could have pulled her into the water."

Granger's face paled, and he avoided Marlowe's gaze. "Maybe," he whispered. "But I didn't see no one else. Just that shadow."

Marlowe leaned in closer. "You're afraid, aren't you? Afraid of what you saw."

Granger's eyes flicked toward the door, as if he were expecting someone to burst in at any moment. "This lake," he said quietly, "it's always been bad luck. People talk about curses, but I've seen things out here—things that don't make sense. I don't know if Charlotte was pushed, or if the lake took her. All I know is that nothing good comes from sticking your nose where it don't belong."

Marlowe straightened, watching Granger closely. The man was clearly frightened, but whether it was fear of the lake's reputation or fear of someone who might have been there that night, Marlowe couldn't be sure. But one thing was certain—Granger's story wasn't complete.

"I appreciate your time, Tom," Marlowe said, his tone neutral. "But if you remember anything else—anything at all—you need to come forward."

Granger nodded weakly, but the detective could tell he wasn't going to be eager to revisit the lake anytime soon.

As Marlowe left the boathouse and made his way back to the shore, his mind churned with questions. Charlotte had been out by the lake that night, and Granger's account of her strange behaviour—her pacing, her trance-like state—suggested she had been troubled, perhaps even frightened. But by what? Or by whom?

And the shadow Granger had seen—had it been real, or just a trick of the light? Had someone else been lurking near the lake, watching Charlotte, waiting for the right moment to act?

Marlowe's instincts told him that Granger knew more than he was letting on. But whether out of fear or superstition, the boatman wasn't ready to reveal everything. Yet.

As the sun dipped lower on the horizon, casting the lake in eerie shadows, Marlowe couldn't shake the feeling that the answers he sought were closer than ever. But they were hidden beneath layers of fear, lies, and perhaps, something more sinister.

Charlotte's death wasn't just a tragic accident. Someone had been there that night. And Marlowe was determined to find out who.

Chapter 17: Letters From the Past

Detective Jonathan Marlowe stood in the dimly lit study of the Winthrop estate, his eyes scanning the rows of leather-bound books that lined the shelves. The heavy scent of old paper and polished wood clung to the air, giving the room an almost oppressive atmosphere. This study, like the rest of the house, seemed frozen in time—a shrine to the Winthrop family's wealth and power. But it was also a place that held secrets, ones that Marlowe was determined to uncover.

Earlier that day, while reviewing some old documents and items from Charlotte's personal effects, Marlowe had come across something unexpected: a small bundle of letters tied with a faded ribbon. The letters had been hidden in the bottom of a wooden chest, beneath stacks of forgotten papers. They were old—yellowed with age—but unmistakably personal. The handwriting on the letters was delicate, almost elegant, but the signature at the bottom of each one had been carefully torn off, leaving the identity of the sender a mystery.

Intrigued, Marlowe had taken the letters back to the estate, determined to find out more. The letters spanned several years, and their content hinted at a past that Charlotte had been hiding—a relationship with someone outside the family, a relationship that had not only caused tension but might have led to the unravelling of everything.

As Marlowe sat down at William Winthrop's large mahogany desk, he untied the bundle and carefully unfolded the first letter. The paper was fragile, and the ink had faded, but the words were still legible.

My Dearest Charlotte,

I cannot begin to express how much I miss you. These stolen moments, though brief, have been my only solace during these dark times. You are the light that has kept me going, the one thing I cherish in this world. But I fear for us, my love. Your father suspects something—he has begun asking questions, and I know that if he discovers the truth, it will tear everything apart.

I cannot bear the thought of losing you, but the weight of this secrecy is becoming too much. I know you love your family, but I need you to think of us, of the future we could have together. Please, meet me at the lake tomorrow night. We need to decide what comes next.

Yours forever,

[Signature torn off]

Marlowe sat back in his chair, absorbing the implications of the letter. This wasn't just a fleeting romance—it had been something serious, something dangerous. Charlotte had been involved with someone, someone her father clearly wouldn't have approved of. But who?

The mention of the lake sent a chill through Marlowe. It seemed to be at the center of everything—a place where secrets had been kept, and now, a place where Charlotte had met her tragic end.

He turned to the next letter.

My Dearest,

It has been weeks since we last saw each other, and I fear we are slipping away. I know your father has tightened his grip on you—he will never allow us to be together, not as long as he controls your future. But you have to understand that we cannot continue living like this. I need you to choose, Charlotte. I need you to find the courage to break free.

I will wait for you at our usual spot by the lake tomorrow night. If you do not come, I will know your decision. I love you, but I cannot live in the shadows any longer.

Yours always,

[Signature torn off]

Marlowe frowned, turning the letter over in his hands. Whoever had written these letters had been deeply in love with Charlotte, but their relationship had been plagued by secrecy and fear. And clearly,

Charlotte had been torn between this person and her family—particularly her father.

The dates on the letters suggested that this relationship had taken place several years ago, long before Charlotte had begun to pull away from her family more publicly. But if William Winthrop had suspected something back then, it could have explained why he had become so controlling over her life in recent years. Perhaps he had tried to sever her connection to this mysterious lover, forcing her deeper into the family business to keep her under his control.

Marlowe turned his attention to the final letter in the bundle. This one seemed more hurried, the handwriting more frantic.

Charlotte,

I cannot wait any longer. You must meet me tonight. I know it's dangerous, but if we don't act now, we will never be free. I overheard your father speaking with his lawyer—he is planning something, something that will ensure you never leave.

If you truly love me, if you want a life outside of the Winthrop legacy, you need to meet me at the lake tonight. We can leave together, far away from here. But if you don't come... I will know it's over. I cannot keep waiting, Charlotte. This is our last chance.

[Signature torn off]

Marlowe's pulse quickened. This last letter had a sense of urgency, almost desperation. Whoever had written it had been ready to run away with Charlotte, to leave behind the life she had been trapped in. And yet, for some reason, it hadn't happened. Charlotte had stayed.

The lake, again. Always the lake.

Marlowe's mind raced. Could it be that Charlotte had intended to leave her family all those years ago, but something—or someone—had stopped her? Could her father have discovered the relationship and put an end to it in a way that went beyond control and intimidation?

There was still one piece missing: the identity of the mysterious lover. Marlowe needed to know who had written these letters. He had a feeling that this affair had played a larger role in Charlotte's fate than anyone had realized.

He carefully refolded the letters and placed them back in the bundle. There was one person who might have the answers he needed—Eleanor Winthrop. Charlotte's mother had seemed fragile during their last interview, but she had been more aware of the family's secrets than she had let on. If anyone knew about this affair, it would be her.

Later that afternoon, Marlowe found himself sitting across from Eleanor Winthrop in the mansion's parlour, the large windows overlooking the lake casting long shadows across the room. Eleanor looked even more fragile than before, her grief weighing heavily on her.

"Mrs. Winthrop," Marlowe began gently, "I need to ask you about Charlotte's past. Specifically, about a relationship she had—one that she kept secret from your husband."

Eleanor's eyes flickered with alarm, but she said nothing, her hands gripping the armrests of her chair tightly.

"I found letters," Marlowe continued, "hidden in Charlotte's belongings. They were written by someone who clearly loved her. Someone who wanted to run away with her."

Eleanor closed her eyes, as if bracing herself for a painful memory. When she finally spoke, her voice was barely a whisper. "I knew."

Marlowe leaned forward. "You knew about the affair?"

Eleanor nodded slowly. "Yes. Charlotte confided in me. She was in love, but William... he would never have allowed it. He was too concerned with the family's reputation, with keeping control of everything—of her."

"Who was the man she was involved with?" Marlowe asked gently.

Eleanor's eyes filled with tears. "His name was Daniel Gresham. He was a young lawyer from a well-to-do family, but not one of the old families, not the kind William wanted Charlotte to marry into.

They met at one of the charity events, and it blossomed from there. But William found out, and after that... everything changed."

"What happened?" Marlowe pressed.

"William threatened him," Eleanor whispered. "He made it clear that if Daniel didn't leave Charlotte alone, he would destroy him—professionally and personally. He told Charlotte that if she didn't end it, she would be cut off from the family entirely."

Marlowe felt a knot tightening in his chest. "And she ended it?"

Eleanor nodded, her voice breaking. "Yes. She was heartbroken, but she felt like she had no choice. William had too much power. She didn't meet Daniel that night at the lake. She stayed, and he left."

Marlowe sat back, absorbing the weight of Eleanor's confession. Charlotte had been forced to give up the one person she had truly loved, all in the name of preserving her family's legacy. And now, years later, she had died at the very place where she was supposed to find freedom.

As Marlowe left the mansion, the pieces of the puzzle began to fall into place. Charlotte's life had been defined by control, by the choices made for her, not by her. And the person who had wielded the most control was her father.

But someone else had been watching from the shadows, someone who knew about her past and might have used it to their advantage.

Marlowe knew that the answers he sought were close—closer than ever. And the truth, once uncovered, would shake the Winthrop family to its core.

Chapter 18: A Fateful Night

Detective Marlowe sat at his desk, the soft hum of the police station punctuated by the occasional phone call or conversation in the background. Before him, a series of documents, notes, and witness interviews were spread across the surface, each piece of information a part of the puzzle that was Charlotte Winthrop's final night.

For weeks, Marlowe had been sifting through the tangled web of family secrets, old affairs, and suspicious behaviour. Now, he had enough threads to start weaving them into a coherent picture of what had happened the night Charlotte died. The challenge was not just to reconstruct her final moments, but to determine who had been responsible for orchestrating her tragic end.

Marlowe took a deep breath and began laying out the timeline in his mind, each piece fitting into place as he mentally replayed that fateful night.

8:00 PM – The Dinner Party

The Winthrop family had gathered for dinner that evening, a formal affair at the estate. Charlotte had been present, though her demeanour had been distant. According to Eleanor Winthrop's recollection, Charlotte barely touched her food, her mind clearly elsewhere. Tensions had been brewing in the family for weeks—particularly between Charlotte and her father, William.

In her final days, Charlotte had been growing more withdrawn, no longer willing to play the role of the dutiful daughter. She had already set her plan in motion, rewriting her will and preparing to leave behind the family's suffocating legacy. But the confrontation between her and her father during dinner had only heightened the pressure.

David, Charlotte's brother, had been there as well, though he had seemed equally preoccupied. In earlier interviews, Marlowe had noted David's nervousness and the simmering resentment between the siblings. David had always been overshadowed by Charlotte, the favoured child, and his financial troubles had left him desperate for control over the family's fortune.

9:30 PM – The Argument

After dinner, things had escalated. Marlowe had pieced together from various sources—including Eleanor and David—that Charlotte and William had argued once again, this time over her plans to distance herself from the family business. William had accused her of betraying the family, and Charlotte, emboldened by her recent decisions, had finally stood her ground.

Eleanor had tried to intervene, but Charlotte had left the room abruptly, retreating to her bedroom. According to Eleanor, Charlotte had been visibly shaken but determined. She had refused to bend to her father's will any longer, a decision that would ultimately set her on a dangerous path.

10:15 PM – The Walk to the Lake

After the argument, Charlotte had gone to her room, but not for long. Based on the evidence Marlowe had gathered—including footprints leading away from the estate and witness accounts—Charlotte had left the house shortly after 10:00 PM. She had taken the familiar path to the lake, the one she had walked countless times before. But this time, it wasn't for solace.

Her destination was the lake, where she had once met Daniel Gresham—the lover she had been forced to abandon years ago. The letters Marlowe had discovered suggested that Charlotte had been reflecting on that lost love, and the lake had always been a symbol of her entrapment and longing for freedom. Perhaps she had intended to leave once and for all, to break free of the chains her father had placed on her life.

But someone else knew she would be there that night.

11:00 PM – The Shadow at the Lake

Tom Granger, the boatman, had been out on the lake, drifting quietly in his boat, when he saw Charlotte pacing by the water's edge.

His account, though evasive and incomplete, had been crucial in establishing that Charlotte had been agitated, perhaps waiting for something—or someone. Granger had mentioned seeing a shadow near the trees, a fleeting glimpse of someone watching Charlotte from the cover of darkness.

Marlowe now believed that shadow had been David.

David's financial struggles had left him in a precarious position. His gambling debts, which Marlowe had discovered through bank records, had mounted to the point where he was in danger of losing everything. With Charlotte's recent decision to rewrite her will and distance herself from the family, David had seen his last chance slipping away. Charlotte was planning to leave, to take her share of the family fortune with her. And if she left, David would be left with nothing.

Marlowe suspected that David had followed Charlotte to the lake, intending to confront her, perhaps to convince her to stay—or to silence her if she refused. The shadow Granger had seen moving in the trees had been David, hiding and waiting for the right moment to act.

11:15 PM – The Confrontation

Charlotte had stood at the water's edge, staring out at the lake, lost in thought. She had been pacing, torn between her desire to leave and the weight of the family's legacy pulling her back. David had approached her then, emerging from the trees. The confrontation that followed was brief but intense. David had likely pleaded with her to reconsider, to stay and help him, but Charlotte had refused. She had been resolute in her decision to leave.

In the heat of the moment, something had gone wrong.

Marlowe suspected that David, desperate and afraid of losing everything, had acted impulsively. Whether it had been an accident or a moment of blind rage, David had pushed Charlotte into the lake. There were no signs of a struggle on the shore, but Charlotte's drowning had not been the clean accident it appeared to be. The autopsy had shown signs of restraint, bruising on her wrists—evidence that someone had held her under the water.

David had panicked. In his desperation, he had fled, leaving Charlotte's body to be discovered later. He had likely believed that the lake's reputation—the old legends of its curse—would cover up his crime. After all, the lake had taken lives before. Who would question another drowning in its dark waters?

12:00 AM – The Aftermath

When Charlotte's body was discovered the next morning, the initial assumption had been that it was a tragic accident. The family had been quick to accept that narrative, particularly William, who had been so focused on protecting the family's legacy that he hadn't considered foul play. Eleanor had been grief-stricken, but she, too, had accepted the idea that Charlotte's death was an accident—perhaps because the alternative was too horrifying to contemplate.

But Marlowe knew better. The pieces had finally come together. David, consumed by jealousy, desperation, and fear, had confronted his sister at the lake, and in that fateful moment, he had ended her life.

As Marlowe finished piecing together the events of that night, he couldn't shake the feeling of unease that settled over him. The truth, though painful, had finally come to light. Charlotte had been caught between two worlds—her desire for freedom and her family's oppressive control. In the end, it had been her brother's desperation that had sealed her fate.

Marlowe stood, gathering the evidence and preparing to confront David. It wouldn't be an easy conversation, but justice demanded that Charlotte's story be told in full.

As he left the station, the weight of the investigation pressing down on him, Marlowe knew that the Winthrop family would never be the same. The secrets they had tried so hard to bury had come to the surface, and now, there was no turning back.

David Winthrop would have to answer for his sister's death.

And the lake, once the symbol of the family's wealth and tranquillity, had become a witness to their darkest truths.

Chapter 19: The Storm

Detective Jonathan Marlowe stood on the shores of the Winthrop family lake, staring out at the water, his mind racing with the implications of the latest evidence. The truth about Charlotte's death was within his grasp—he could feel it—but there was still something missing, a key detail that would tie everything together.

The wind picked up, rustling the leaves of the trees lining the lake, and Marlowe couldn't help but think about the storm that had swept through the region the night Charlotte died. It had been sudden and violent, a thunderstorm that had seemingly come out of nowhere, lashing the estate with rain and wind for hours. It was one of the first things the locals had mentioned to him when he started his investigation, but at the time, he had thought little of it.

Now, as he stood there, the storm took on new significance. Could it have hidden something vital? Could it have erased or obscured the final clues that would reveal what really happened to Charlotte?

Marlowe's mind returned to the timeline he had reconstructed. He knew Charlotte had walked to the lake late that night, sometime after 10:00 PM, but the storm had rolled in soon after. Witnesses had described how the wind had howled through the trees, and the rain had come down in sheets, making visibility nearly impossible. Tom Granger, the boatman, had mentioned how the storm had driven him off the water, forcing him to row back to the boathouse earlier than he'd planned.

It was possible that the storm had not only driven away potential witnesses but had also washed away evidence—footprints, markings on the ground, or even items Charlotte may have had with her. Marlowe's frustration deepened as he realized just how much the storm had complicated his investigation.

He turned toward Suarez, who was standing a few feet away, watching him with a thoughtful expression. "The storm," Marlowe muttered, shaking his head. "It might've destroyed some of the most important evidence."

Suarez nodded, frowning. "I've been thinking the same thing. It's too convenient, isn't it? Everything we know about Charlotte's last movements leads us here, but whatever happened by the lake was almost completely wiped away by that storm. No clear footprints, no sign of a struggle—nothing."

Marlowe exhaled sharply, feeling the weight of the investigation press down on him. "If there was a confrontation here, or if David or anyone else met her, the storm could have washed away the clues."

Suarez tilted her head thoughtfully. "But storms can also stir things up—move evidence to unexpected places. If something was dropped or left behind, it could've been blown or carried by the water to another part of the shore."

Marlowe turned, scanning the area around the lake once again, this time with a more determined focus. The storm had raged through, but perhaps not everything had been erased. There might still be something hidden, displaced by the storm.

"Let's search the shoreline again," Marlowe said, his voice filled with renewed determination. "We need to comb through every inch of this place. There has to be something we missed."

For the next hour, Marlowe and Suarez meticulously searched the edges of the lake, their eyes trained on the ground, the rocks, and the tall grass that grew along the water's edge. The area was still muddy in places from the rainstorm, and the damp earth held the faintest impressions of disturbed ground, but it was difficult to determine if any of it was recent or simply remnants of the storm's fury.

They had just about given up when Suarez suddenly called out, her voice sharp with excitement. "Marlowe! Over here!"

Marlowe hurried over to where Suarez was crouched near a dense thicket of bushes. In her hand, she held a small, mud-streaked object, carefully dusting it off with her gloved fingers.

"It's a locket," she said, holding it up to the light. The silver locket was tarnished and partially covered in mud, but the intricate design was unmistakable—a family heirloom, much like the other pieces of jewellery Charlotte had been known to wear.

Marlowe took the locket from Suarez, inspecting it carefully. "It must've been Charlotte's," he said, flipping it over to examine the back. "But how did it end up all the way over here?"

Suarez looked around, piecing it together. "The storm. The wind and rain could've knocked it off, or maybe she dropped it during the struggle. Either way, the storm probably carried it away from the actual scene."

Marlowe opened the locket carefully. Inside, there was a small photograph of a young woman—Charlotte—and a faded image of a man Marlowe didn't recognize immediately. But the way the locket had been carefully placed, as though Charlotte had cherished it, suggested this man had meant something to her.

"Do you recognize him?" Suarez asked, peering at the photograph.

Marlowe studied the image for a moment, and then it clicked. It was Daniel Gresham, the man from the letters—the one Charlotte had once planned to run away with.

"It's him," Marlowe said, his voice low. "Daniel Gresham. This locket could be the key. Charlotte must've been thinking about him that night—maybe even planning to finally leave for good."

Suarez frowned. "But if she was planning to leave, why would she have stayed long enough to be confronted? And by who?"

Marlowe's mind churned with possibilities. The locket indicated that Charlotte had been thinking of her past, possibly rekindling her desire for freedom. But if David—or someone else—had followed her to the lake that night, determined to stop her from leaving, it would explain the sudden confrontation that led to her death.

"The storm may have covered up the physical evidence," Marlowe said, pocketing the locket, "but it can't cover up motive. David must've known she was planning to leave—maybe he saw this locket or overheard something that pushed him to act."

Suarez nodded, her expression serious. "So, what's next? We've got the locket, we've got the history between David and Charlotte, and we've got the timeline. But we still need a confession."

Marlowe stared out at the lake, the wind rustling through the trees once more. "It's time to confront David. We know he was there, we know he had the most to lose if Charlotte left, and now we have this."

As they prepared to leave the lake, the storm that had once obscured the truth began to feel less like an obstacle and more like a crucial turning point in the case. The wind and rain had carried away the physical clues, but it had also stirred up something far more valuable—Charlotte's secret plans, her lost love, and the motive that had led to her tragic end.

And now, it was time to bring the truth to the surface.

Back at the Winthrop estate, Marlowe felt the tension in the air as he approached David's quarters. The family was unravelling—William was still seething after the will reading, and Eleanor's grief had left her in a state of withdrawal. But David? David had been conspicuously absent ever since the investigation had taken a darker turn.

Marlowe knocked on David's door, his heart pounding. There was no response.

He knocked again, more forcefully this time. "David, it's Detective Marlowe. We need to talk."

After a moment, the door creaked open, revealing David standing in the doorway, his face pale, his eyes rimmed with exhaustion. There was something off about him—something nervous, twitchy.

"What do you want?" David asked, his voice barely hiding the tremor beneath it.

Marlowe stepped inside, his eyes locked on David's. "We found something near the lake. A locket."

David's face drained of color, and he took a step back. "A... a locket? I don't know anything about that."

Marlowe's gaze didn't waver. "It belonged to Charlotte. It was found near where she died. And I think you know exactly how it got there."

David's eyes flicked to the door, as if calculating an escape, but Marlowe stood his ground.

"It's time to tell the truth, David," Marlowe said firmly. "You were there that night. You followed her to the lake. And when she refused to stay, when she told you she was leaving for good... you panicked, didn't you?"

David's lip trembled, his hands balling into fists at his sides. "You don't know what you're talking about."

"Don't I?" Marlowe pressed. "I know she was planning to leave the family behind, just like she planned to years ago. And I know you couldn't let her do it—not when it meant losing everything."

David's composure crumbled in an instant, and he slumped against the wall, burying his face in his hands. "I didn't mean to do it," he whispered, his voice breaking. "It all happened so fast. I just... I just wanted to talk to her. But she wouldn't listen. She said she was leaving—she said she didn't care what happened to me. I couldn't... I couldn't let her walk away like that."

Marlowe's heart sank as David's confession spilled out. "So you pushed her."

David nodded, tears streaming down his face. "I didn't mean to, I swear. But when she fell into the water, I didn't know what to do. I panicked. The storm... the storm was so loud, no one could hear anything. I thought... I thought the lake would cover it up. That no one would know."

But the storm hadn't covered it up. Not completely. And now, Marlowe had the truth.

As he led David out of the room, the weight of the case finally settling on his shoulders, Marlowe knew that Charlotte's story would finally be told.

The storm had taken many things that night. But it hadn't taken justice.

Chapter 20: Family Betrayals

The Winthrop estate, usually a symbol of unshakable wealth and legacy, felt like it was teetering on the edge of collapse. Detective Marlowe sat at the head of the grand dining table, the same table where, just weeks ago, the Winthrop family had dined in cold silence, concealing their fractured relationships behind layers of formality. Now, however, the polite veneer had cracked.

After David's tearful confession about Charlotte's death, the fragile truce that held the family together was broken, and tensions that had been simmering for years began to boil over.

As Marlowe waited for the family members to gather for one last, difficult confrontation, he reflected on how the case had unfolded. Charlotte's tragic death had been the catalyst for the family's unravelling, but the true roots of their betrayal ran much deeper.

William Winthrop was the first to arrive, his imposing figure stiff with barely-contained fury. He sat at the opposite end of the table, his eyes fixed on Marlowe with an air of cold defiance. The patriarch had lost everything—his daughter, his control over the family, and soon, it seemed, his carefully constructed legacy.

Moments later, Eleanor Winthrop entered, her face pale and gaunt, but her posture surprisingly resolute. Since Charlotte's death, she had retreated into herself, wracked by grief and guilt. But today, there was a certain strength in her eyes, as if she had finally decided to confront the reality of her family's deep betrayals.

Finally, David, the youngest of the Winthrop children and now a broken man, shuffled into the room, his head hung low. The confession he had made about accidentally killing Charlotte had lifted the weight of secrecy from his shoulders, but it had also shattered his already precarious standing in the family. His father had not spoken a word to him since that night.

The tension in the room was suffocating as Marlowe looked around, waiting for the inevitable confrontation. He could sense that the air was thick with unspoken accusations and buried resentments. But now, with the truth out in the open, Marlowe suspected that the family's hidden betrayals would finally come to light.

He stood up, clearing his throat. "We need to discuss what comes next," Marlowe said evenly, his gaze sweeping the room. "David has confessed to pushing Charlotte into the lake during an argument, but there's more to this story. This family has been carrying secrets, and it's time for them to come out."

William's eyes narrowed, his voice a low growl. "What more is there to say, Detective? My son killed my daughter. Isn't that enough?"

David flinched, his hands shaking slightly. Eleanor shot a cold glance at her husband, her voice trembling with emotion. "Don't act like you're innocent in all of this, William. You've been controlling and manipulating us for years. Everything in this family revolves around you and your precious legacy. That's why Charlotte wanted to leave in the first place."

Marlowe remained silent, allowing the conversation to unravel. This was what he had been waiting for—the hidden resentments rising to the surface.

William's face darkened, his voice laced with anger. "I did what I had to do to protect this family. Charlotte was being reckless—she was throwing everything away for her selfish desires. She didn't understand the responsibility that comes with being a Winthrop."

Eleanor's voice sharpened. "Responsibility? You mean control. You controlled every aspect of her life, and now she's dead because of it."

David, his voice weak, finally spoke. "She didn't want any of this, Dad. She was planning to leave, and you... you couldn't handle that. You pushed her too hard."

William slammed his fist on the table, his face red with fury. "You dare to blame me? You were the one who killed her, David! You were the one who couldn't let her go!"

David's eyes welled with tears, but he didn't respond. The accusation hung in the air like a poisonous cloud, and Marlowe knew it was time to intervene.

"I think it's time we talked about what really tore this family apart," Marlowe said, his voice calm but firm. "This isn't just about Charlotte's death. It's about betrayal, blackmail, and hidden agendas that have been festering for years."

William's cold stare shifted to Marlowe, but the detective remained steady. He pulled out a small folder from his briefcase and placed it on the table.

"I've uncovered some interesting documents in the course of this investigation," Marlowe began. "Financial records, personal correspondence, and legal agreements that show this family has been at war with itself long before Charlotte's death."

He opened the folder and slid a few pages across the table toward William. "Let's start with your business dealings, William. You've been funnelling money into secret offshore accounts for years, hiding assets not only from the public but from your own family. You've used blackmail, threats, and under-the-table deals to maintain control, all while keeping Eleanor and David in the dark."

Eleanor's eyes widened, and she looked at her husband in horror. "Is this true?"

William didn't deny it, his jaw set in a grim line. "I did what was necessary to keep this family strong."

"Strong?" Eleanor said, her voice cracking. "You lied to us. You manipulated us."

Marlowe continued, ignoring William's defensive posture. "But it wasn't just about money. I found letters—correspondence between you and a former business partner, Richard Caldwell. It seems there was an agreement to cut David out of the family business if things didn't go according to plan. You were willing to sacrifice your own son to protect the company."

David's face went pale as he stared at his father, disbelief etched in every feature. "You... you were going to cut me out?"

William's silence was damning.

Eleanor stood from her chair, her voice rising. "You've destroyed everything, William. Charlotte is dead, and now you've betrayed your own son. Was there ever a line you wouldn't cross?"

Marlowe gave her a small nod, knowing that she was finally seeing the full extent of her husband's deceptions. But he wasn't finished.

"There's more," Marlowe said, his tone darkening. "Charlotte knew about these betrayals. She discovered the truth about your offshore accounts, William, and she was planning to expose you. That's why she rewrote her will—she wanted to leave the family business behind and create a foundation with her inheritance. You knew that if she left, your empire would crumble."

William's face contorted with rage. "That little fool had no idea what she was doing!"

Marlowe shook his head. "She knew exactly what she was doing. She was trying to free herself from you."

Eleanor stepped forward, her voice cold. "You couldn't control her anymore, William. That's why you pushed her so hard. You didn't care about her happiness—you only cared about your legacy."

David, still reeling from the revelations, stood as well, his voice shaky but resolute. "And you never cared about me, either. All I ever wanted was to matter—to be seen as more than just the second son. But I was never enough for you."

William's furious gaze shifted to his son. "You were weak, David. I gave you every opportunity, and you squandered it. You're no better than Charlotte, always chasing your own desires instead of thinking about the family."

The room fell into a heavy silence as the weight of William's betrayals settled over the family. He had manipulated, blackmailed, and controlled them for years, all in the name of maintaining power. But in the end, it had cost him everything.

Marlowe stepped forward, his voice quiet but commanding. "This family has been built on lies and betrayal, but now the truth is out. Charlotte died because of the pressure and control you placed on her, William. And David acted out of desperation because he knew he could never live up to your expectations."

William slumped in his chair, the fight leaving him. For the first time, he seemed to realize just how much he had lost—not only his daughter but the loyalty of the people closest to him.

Eleanor turned away from her husband, tears in her eyes. David remained silent, his shoulders slumped in defeat.

As Marlowe watched the fractured family before him, he knew that the Winthrop empire had finally fallen. The truth had been exposed, and the betrayals that had torn them apart were laid bare for all to see.

Charlotte's death had been the tragic consequence of a family consumed by its own ambitions and secrets. And now, as the pieces of the puzzle fell into place, Marlowe could see that this was not just a story of one woman's death—it was the story of a family destroyed by its own greed and deceit.

The Winthrops had betrayed each other for years.

And in the end, it had cost them everything.

Chapter 21: The Lawyer's Secret

The afternoon sun filtered through the large windows of the Winthrop estate's study, casting long shadows across the room where Detective Marlowe sat with Henry Lawson, the family's long-serving lawyer. Lawson's usually calm demeanour was strained, his hands fidgeting as he adjusted his glasses and leaned forward in his chair. It was clear that he had something weighing on his mind—something important.

Marlowe had suspected for a while that Lawson knew more than he had let on. As the family's lawyer, he had been deeply involved in the affairs of the Winthrops, privy to their secrets, financial dealings, and personal battles. Up until now, Lawson had maintained his professional distance, revealing only what was required. But as the investigation into Charlotte's death had reached a boiling point, it seemed Lawson had decided that keeping silent was no longer an option.

"I appreciate you meeting with me again, Mr. Lawson," Marlowe began, his tone neutral but probing. "There's been a lot of information surfacing about the Winthrop family in the last few days. I'm starting to piece things together, but I get the sense that there's more—something you haven't told me yet."

Lawson exhaled deeply, his fingers tapping rhythmically on the armrest of his chair. He looked out the window for a long moment before finally speaking. "Detective, you have to understand—I've served the Winthrop family for over three decades. My role has always been to protect their interests, both legally and personally. But what's happening now... I can't keep quiet anymore."

Marlowe raised an eyebrow, intrigued. He had always assumed Lawson was fiercely loyal to William Winthrop, the family patriarch, but something had shifted. Lawson seemed conflicted, torn between his duty as a lawyer and his conscience as a human being.

"What is it you're holding back?" Marlowe asked, leaning forward slightly, his voice firm but patient.

Lawson swallowed hard, his eyes darting back to meet Marlowe's. "There are documents—legal documents—that I've kept hidden at the family's request. Some of them concern Charlotte, and others involve William's financial dealings. But there's one document in particular... something that could change everything."

Marlowe's pulse quickened. "Go on."

Lawson hesitated, then reached into his briefcase, pulling out a thick envelope sealed with an old-fashioned wax stamp. He placed it on the desk between them, his hand hovering over it for a moment before finally pushing it toward Marlowe.

"This," Lawson said, his voice barely above a whisper, "is Charlotte's original will. The one she had drawn up before she made any changes."

Marlowe's brow furrowed. "The original will? Why wasn't this included in the official documentation?"

"Because William made sure it wasn't," Lawson replied grimly. "Charlotte had made a decision years ago, long before her most recent will—one that her father would never have approved of. She wanted to leave everything to her brother, David. Every cent of her inheritance, all her shares in the family business, everything."

Marlowe sat back, processing this new information. Charlotte had originally intended to leave her entire fortune to David? That was a major revelation, one that didn't align with the fractured relationship between the siblings he had come to know. But the decision to rewrite the will, favouring a charitable foundation instead, had come later—after something had clearly changed.

"Why did she change her will?" Marlowe asked, narrowing his eyes. "What happened between her and David?"

Lawson sighed. "That's where things get complicated. Charlotte and David were close once—very close. She wanted him to take over the family business, to share in the responsibility. But over the years, David's personal issues—his gambling, his recklessness—pushed them apart. He became resentful of her, believing she was the favoured child, and that resentment grew into something much darker."

Marlowe's mind churned with possibilities. This new information about Charlotte's original will added a whole new layer of complexity to the case. It explained why David might have been desperate to stop Charlotte from leaving or rewriting her will again. But there was still more to uncover.

"And William?" Marlowe asked. "What role did he play in all of this?"

Lawson's expression darkened. "William found out about the original will before Charlotte ever had a chance to implement it. He confronted her, and that's when everything began to unravel. He pressured her to change the will, to keep control over the family fortune and the business. He didn't trust David to handle the responsibility, and in his eyes, Charlotte was the only one capable of carrying on the family's legacy. That's when she made the second will, cutting David out and leaving most of the estate to the foundation."

Marlowe rubbed his temples, the weight of the revelations settling in. William's need for control had not only caused friction between him and Charlotte, but it had also driven a wedge between her and David. David, once the intended heir to her fortune, had been left with nothing, and that betrayal had festered in the years leading up to Charlotte's death.

"Why are you telling me this now?" Marlowe asked, eyeing Lawson carefully. "You've kept these documents hidden for years. What changed?"

Lawson leaned forward, his face filled with a mixture of guilt and determination. "Because Charlotte's death wasn't just a tragic accident. It was the result of years of manipulation, lies, and power struggles within the family. I've served the Winthrops loyally, but I can't stand by any longer. William's greed, David's resentment—it's all led to this. And I need to make sure the truth comes out."

Marlowe nodded, appreciating Lawson's honesty. The lawyer had become an unlikely ally, and his willingness to break his silence meant that the final pieces of the puzzle were now falling into place. But there was one last question that lingered in Marlowe's mind.

"Does William know you have this?" Marlowe asked, tapping the envelope containing the original will.

Lawson shook his head. "No. William believes the original will was destroyed years ago. He doesn't know I kept a copy hidden all this time."

Marlowe's jaw tightened. "And if he finds out?"

Lawson's face hardened. "He won't. Not if we act quickly."

Marlowe stood, pocketing the envelope, his mind racing with the implications of this new discovery. The original will had revealed a side of Charlotte's intentions that no one in the family had anticipated. She had once placed her trust in David, only to be forced into rewriting her future by her father's iron grip. That betrayal had set the stage for everything that had followed.

As Marlowe prepared to leave, Lawson called out one last warning. "Be careful, Detective. William won't go down without a fight. He's been pulling the strings for years, and if he thinks he's about to lose control, he'll do whatever it takes to protect himself."

Marlowe gave a grim nod. "I'll be ready."

Back at the station, Marlowe sat at his desk, unfolding the contents of the envelope once more. The original will laid out in clear terms what Charlotte had once intended: her entire fortune, every asset she owned, was to be left to David Winthrop. It was a stark contrast to the more recent will, which diverted most of her wealth to charity.

The betrayal must have been a bitter blow to David. To know that at one point he had been the chosen heir, only to lose everything because of his father's interference—it explained his desperation, his sense of injustice. And now, with Charlotte gone, the question of inheritance had become even more fraught.

Marlowe's mind churned with the implications. The revelation of the original will shifted the dynamics of the entire case. It provided David with a clear motive for wanting to stop Charlotte from leaving, but it also cast William in an even more dangerous light. He had manipulated his children for years, turning them against each other in his quest to control the family legacy.

But there was one thing Marlowe couldn't shake: Lawson's warning. William Winthrop wasn't a man to go down easily, and with the truth about his manipulations coming to light, Marlowe knew that the final confrontation was approaching.

As the clock ticked toward the end of the investigation, Marlowe prepared for the storm that was about to break. The family lawyer's secret had changed everything—and now, the truth was poised to tear the Winthrop family apart once and for all.

And in the end, justice for Charlotte would be the final blow.

Chapter 22: The Heir's Alibi

The soft hum of the station's fluorescent lights filled the silence as Detective Marlowe sat at his desk, reviewing the notes from the ongoing investigation. After discovering Charlotte's original will and the hidden motives it exposed, Marlowe's focus had shifted. The tangled web of family secrets and betrayals had left every member of the Winthrop family under suspicion. But now, it was time to carefully reexamine the details of that fateful night—specifically, the alibis.

Marlowe had already spoken to each family member, and their alibis had seemed straightforward at the time. But in light of recent revelations, something gnawed at him. The timelines, the gaps in their stories, and their movements the night Charlotte died—they no longer seemed as airtight as before.

He picked up the reports, starting with David Winthrop, the heir who had lost everything. David's confession of accidentally pushing Charlotte had provided some clarity, but it didn't explain everything. Marlowe had believed, at first, that David had acted alone in a moment of desperation. But now, as he dug deeper, he began to wonder if there was more to the story—if David had been manipulated, or if he wasn't being entirely truthful.

Marlowe tapped his pen on the desk, considering the possibilities. It was time to revisit each alibi and look at them through a new lens.

William Winthrop had been the first to offer his alibi. According to him, after the argument with Charlotte, he had retired to his study for the evening and hadn't left until well after midnight. He claimed to have been reading and making notes on some business documents, completely unaware of Charlotte's movements until the following morning when her body was found.

Marlowe had found it strange that William, who was normally so controlling, had simply let Charlotte storm off without following up on their argument. But at the time, there had been no evidence to contradict his story. Now, with the revelation of his manipulation and the original will, Marlowe began to suspect that William's alibi might be a fabrication—a way to distance himself from the events of that night.

There were no witnesses to confirm William's story. No one had seen him after the argument, and the study, located in a far corner of the estate, was isolated from the rest of the house. William could have easily slipped out unnoticed. But what was his motive? Did he see Charlotte's decision to leave as a final threat to his control over the family? Or had he simply pushed David to act, knowing the young man's fragile emotional state?

Next was Eleanor Winthrop, Charlotte's grief-stricken mother. Eleanor had been vague about her whereabouts that night, claiming to have gone to bed early after the family argument. She admitted that she had heard the storm raging outside and had briefly checked on Charlotte when she noticed her daughter's room was empty, but when she didn't find her, she assumed Charlotte had gone for a walk to cool off, as she sometimes did.

Eleanor had seemed sincere, her grief palpable, but Marlowe couldn't ignore the fact that she had known about Charlotte's past relationship with Daniel Gresham and the pressure William had placed on their daughter. Could Eleanor have played a role in Charlotte's death, whether directly or indirectly? Was it possible that she had turned a blind eye to her husband's manipulations?

Marlowe shook his head. While Eleanor's alibi wasn't solid, he sensed her involvement was more likely rooted in guilt than in any direct action. Still, he couldn't fully rule her out.

Finally, Marlowe came to David's alibi—the one that now raised the most questions. David had confessed to pushing Charlotte into the lake, but his story had left too many gaps. He had claimed that after the family argument, he had gone for a walk around the estate, trying to clear his head. According to him, he had seen Charlotte by the lake, and their confrontation had escalated quickly, resulting in her accidental fall.

But something about David's timeline didn't sit right with Marlowe.

David had claimed the confrontation took place shortly after 11:00 PM, but there was no way to verify that exact time. Tom Granger, the boatman, had placed Charlotte near the lake earlier that night, closer to 10:30 PM, but Granger hadn't mentioned seeing David until much later. If David had been lurking by the lake earlier, why hadn't Granger seen him? And why had David's story changed slightly with each retelling?

Moreover, the discovery of the original will suggested that David had known for years that he was once the intended heir. When Charlotte changed her will, cutting him out and leaving her fortune to charity, it must have fuelled his resentment. His alibi had been a story of panic and impulsiveness, but Marlowe now suspected that David had carefully planned his confrontation with Charlotte, knowing that it was his last chance to reclaim what he believed was rightfully his.

But was David the only one responsible? Marlowe couldn't shake the feeling that he had been manipulated—that someone else had planted the seeds of doubt and desperation in his mind, pushing him toward his fateful encounter with Charlotte.

Marlowe stood, pacing the room as the pieces began to fall into place. Each family member's alibi was shaky, but it was David's that now seemed the most suspicious. His confession had been too convenient, too neatly wrapped in the idea of a tragic accident. But with William's manipulative tendencies, the betrayal over the will, and David's financial desperation, Marlowe could see how the young man might have been driven to act out of more than just impulsive anger.

He sat back down, pulling out his phone. It was time to revisit David one last time—to confront him with the inconsistencies in his alibi and to see if he would finally break under pressure.

Later that afternoon, Marlowe found himself once again in the dimly lit room where David had been staying. The air was thick with tension as David sat across from him, his eyes downcast and his posture slumped. He looked like a man who had been carrying a heavy burden for too long.

"You said you saw Charlotte by the lake around 11:00 PM," Marlowe began, his voice calm but firm. "But the timeline doesn't add up. Tom Granger saw her earlier, and he didn't see you. Why is that?"

David's eyes flickered with uncertainty, but he didn't answer.

Marlowe leaned forward, his gaze intense. "David, I've reviewed all the evidence, and your alibi doesn't match up. You weren't just walking by the lake to clear your head. You were there for a reason, and I think you knew exactly what you were going to do when you found Charlotte."

David swallowed hard, his hands gripping the armrests of his chair. "I... I didn't mean to—"

"I know you didn't mean to kill her," Marlowe interrupted, his voice softening slightly. "But you wanted to stop her from leaving. You knew she was planning to go, to take everything away. And you couldn't let that happen."

Tears welled in David's eyes as he stared down at his hands. "I... I couldn't lose her. I couldn't lose everything. She was going to leave, and I was going to be left with nothing. I just wanted her to listen, but she wouldn't. She was done with all of us. With me."

Marlowe remained silent, letting David's words hang in the air.

"I didn't plan to hurt her," David whispered, his voice breaking. "But when she said she was leaving, that she didn't care what happened to me... I snapped. I pushed her. I thought... I thought she'd be fine. But the storm, the water—it all happened so fast."

David's confession mirrored his earlier statement, but now, Marlowe sensed a deeper truth. The confrontation had been about more than just a sibling argument—it had been about years of betrayal, disappointment, and manipulation.

And while David had been the one to push Charlotte into the lake, he wasn't the only one responsible.

As Marlowe left the room, the weight of the Winthrop family's betrayals settled over him. William's ruthless control, Eleanor's complicity, and David's desperation had all led to Charlotte's tragic death. But there was one final truth that Marlowe couldn't ignore: each member of the family had played a part in her demise.

Now, with David's alibi shattered and the full story of the Winthrop family's corruption exposed, Marlowe knew that justice for Charlotte was finally within reach.

But the damage had already been done. The Winthrops had betrayed each other, and in doing so, they had destroyed the very legacy they had fought so hard to protect.

In the end, there were no winners.

Only the truth.

Chapter 23: Ghosts in the Portraits

The grand hall of the Winthrop estate was dimly lit, the afternoon light filtering through the tall, stained-glass windows and casting shadows across the aged portraits that lined the walls. Detective Jonathan Marlowe stood in the center of the room, his gaze drawn to the haunting eyes of the past generations of the Winthrop family. Each painting, hung with care, depicted stern-faced men and elegant women, their expressions frozen in time, yet somehow still watching over the crumbling legacy of their descendants.

Marlowe had returned to the estate not to interrogate, but to explore the roots of the family's tragedies. The recent revelations—Charlotte's rewritten will, David's confession, and the fractured dynamics between the family members—had painted a picture of a family unravelling. But Marlowe had a nagging feeling that there was something deeper, something embedded in the very history of the Winthrops themselves.

He turned to the first portrait, a large oil painting of Margaret Winthrop, who had drowned in the same lake nearly a century ago. Margaret's story had become part of the estate's folklore—a tragic tale of a woman found floating in the dark waters after a mysterious late-night argument with her husband. The official cause of death had been ruled an accident, but the locals had always whispered about something darker.

Marlowe stepped closer to the portrait, examining the fine details of Margaret's face. She had the same high cheekbones and sharp eyes as Charlotte, a family resemblance that sent a chill down Marlowe's spine. There was something almost eerie about the way Margaret's eyes seemed to follow him across the room.

Turning away, Marlowe walked down the line of portraits, each generation of the Winthrop family seemingly plagued by its own misfortunes. He had read about them in the town's archives—deaths, scandals, and betrayals stretching back for centuries. The more he learned, the more he realized that the Winthrops had always been haunted, not by ghosts, but by their own relentless pursuit of power and control.

Marlowe's steps echoed as he crossed the marble floor to a large oak table in the corner of the hall. Upon it lay a collection of old family journals, brought out from the estate's archives by Eleanor Winthrop. The journals, some worn with age, others more recent, were a record of the family's personal history, written in their own hand.

Marlowe sat down at the table and opened the first journal, dated 1923. It was written by Harold Winthrop, Margaret's husband, and detailed the events leading up to her death. The entries started innocuously enough—business dealings, the family's social life—but as the weeks passed, the tone grew darker, more agitated. Harold wrote of arguments with Margaret, of her growing desire to leave the estate and take their young son with her.

August 12, 1923

Margaret has become more distant. She talks of leaving, of wanting something different for our son. She doesn't understand the burden we carry—the responsibility of maintaining the family name. It is our legacy, our duty. But she refuses to listen.

August 15, 1923

I fear something is happening to her. She wanders by the lake at night, as if drawn to it. She says the water calls to her, that it is a place of peace, but I cannot shake the feeling that something terrible will happen if she continues. She is no longer the woman I married.

Marlowe felt a strange sense of déjà vu as he read Harold's words. Margaret, like Charlotte, had felt trapped by the expectations of her family and had sought solace by the lake. Both women had been suffocated by the legacy of the Winthrop name, and both had met their ends in the dark waters of the lake.

As Marlowe turned the pages, the entries stopped abruptly on August 20, the day Margaret's body had been found. There was no further mention of her death, no reflection from Harold on the tragedy. It was as if the family had buried the truth along with Margaret, choosing instead to move on and continue the cycle of control and repression.

Marlowe set the journal aside and picked up another, this one from the 1960s. It belonged to Evelyn Winthrop, a distant relative who had lived on the estate during a similarly dark time in the family's history. Evelyn's entries were filled with a sense of dread, much like Harold's, though her focus was on the estate itself—particularly the lake.

October 7, 1965

There is something wrong with this place. I feel it every time I walk by the lake. The others don't seem to notice, but I do. The air is heavier there, the shadows longer. And the water... it's so dark. Sometimes I think I see things moving beneath the surface.

October 10, 1965

They don't believe me, but I've seen it. At night, when the moon is high, I've seen figures standing by the lake—women in white, just standing there, staring into the water. Margaret's ghost, they say. But I know better. It's not just her. The lake holds all of them—the ones who never escaped.

Marlowe leaned back in his chair, his mind racing. The lake, which had claimed both Margaret and Charlotte, seemed to be a focal point for the family's tragedies. Evelyn's entries, while filled with superstition, hinted at something deeper—a pattern of death and despair tied to the water, to the Winthrop family's inability to break free from their own legacy.

But it wasn't just the lake. It was the family itself. The journals painted a picture of a lineage bound by control, manipulation, and betrayal, stretching back generations. Each generation had its own tragedies, its own secrets, but they all seemed to share the same fate: the inability to escape the pressures of the family name.

As Marlowe closed the journals and stood, he walked back to the portraits, staring at each face, each pair of eyes that had witnessed the slow unravelling of the Winthrop dynasty.

Margaret Winthrop had been the first, drowning in the lake after an argument with her husband.

Evelyn Winthrop had seen the ghostly figures by the water, claiming that the lake held the souls of those who could never escape the family's grip.

And now, Charlotte Winthrop had become the latest victim—another woman drawn to the lake, another soul trapped by the weight of the family's expectations.

Marlowe stepped closer to Charlotte's portrait, her eyes eerily similar to Margaret's, as if the two women were bound by more than just blood. He couldn't help but feel the weight of their shared history, the chilling parallels that stretched across time.

Was it merely coincidence, or was there something more sinister at play? Was the lake cursed, as the townspeople believed? Or was the true curse the Winthrop name itself—a legacy so poisoned by greed and control that it destroyed everyone who bore it?

As Marlowe turned to leave the grand hall, he knew that the answer to Charlotte's death was not just about the present. It was about the past—about the ghosts in the portraits, the hidden stories in the journals, and the weight of a family history that had been carefully buried for too long.

The truth was not just about who had killed Charlotte—it was about why the Winthrop family had been doomed to repeat the same tragedies over and over again.

And now, it was time to break the cycle.

Chapter 24: Financial Ruin

Detective Jonathan Marlowe sat in his office, the sound of rain tapping against the windowpane, as he poured over the mountain of financial records spread across his desk. The investigation had taken an unexpected turn with the discovery of Charlotte's original will and the intricate family betrayals that followed. But now, a new angle was emerging—one that could explain the desperation and motives behind the events leading up to Charlotte's death: financial ruin.

For years, the Winthrop family had been synonymous with wealth and power. Their sprawling estate, their lavish charity galas, and their influence in business circles had solidified their position at the top of society. But as Marlowe dug deeper into the family's financial records, a different picture began to emerge—one that was far from the glamorous facade the Winthrops had projected.

Marlowe flipped through the most recent tax filings and business ledgers. The signs were subtle at first, but as he cross-referenced the documents with public records and banking statements, the truth became clear. The family fortune wasn't what it seemed. In fact, it was crumbling.

The first major red flag had come when Marlowe had begun investigating William Winthrop's offshore accounts. What had initially seemed like shrewd financial manoeuvring turned out to be a desperate attempt to protect the family's remaining assets from impending collapse. William had been funnelling money into these secret accounts for years, but not out of greed—out of necessity. The Winthrop business empire was on the brink of financial ruin.

The company, once a powerhouse in real estate and development, had been haemorrhaging money due to poor investments, market downturns, and costly legal battles. To maintain the illusion of wealth, William had been moving assets around, taking out loans, and leveraging the family's properties, all while keeping the truth hidden from his children—and, perhaps, even from his wife, Eleanor.

But Charlotte had discovered the truth.

Marlowe's mind raced as he pieced together the timeline. Charlotte, always sharp and insightful, had likely stumbled upon the family's precarious financial situation when she began taking a more active role in managing her personal affairs. Her discovery of the financial instability could have been the real reason she had rewritten her will—choosing to leave her fortune to charity rather than entrusting it to a sinking ship.

As Marlowe pored over the details, a troubling pattern emerged: David had been siphoning money from the family business as well. His gambling debts, which Marlowe had uncovered earlier, were only the tip of the iceberg. David had been secretly embezzling funds from the company, desperate to cover his losses and maintain his extravagant lifestyle. William had known about it but had kept it quiet, preferring to handle the matter privately rather than expose the family to public scandal.

But David's actions had pushed the company even closer to the edge, accelerating the financial collapse that William had been trying so hard to stave off. With both father and son complicit in the mismanagement of the family fortune, Charlotte had found herself caught in the middle of a financial disaster waiting to happen.

Marlowe stood and walked to the window, watching the rain as it poured down over the city. The truth was becoming clear: financial desperation had been the driving force behind much of the family's recent turmoil. And now, he had to consider the possibility that it had led to murder.

Unmasking the Motives

Marlowe returned to his desk, laying out the key players and their potential motives:

William Winthrop, the patriarch, had been desperately trying to protect the family legacy from financial ruin. When Charlotte discovered the truth and rewrote her will, it threatened everything. If she left and took her inheritance with her, the fragile house of cards William had built would collapse. Was it possible that William, in his desperation, had orchestrated Charlotte's death to prevent her from leaving and exposing the family's financial collapse?

David Winthrop, the troubled son, had even more personal reasons for wanting Charlotte out of the way. Not only had Charlotte's rewritten will excluded him from her fortune, but her departure could have exposed his embezzlement and gambling debts to the public. David had already confessed to pushing Charlotte in a moment of panic, but was that the whole story? Could his actions have been fuelled by a more calculated desire to stop her from revealing the family's financial ruin?

Eleanor Winthrop, the grieving mother, had seemed unaware of the full extent of the family's financial troubles. But Marlowe couldn't shake the feeling that Eleanor had known more than she let on. Was it possible that she, too, had been complicit in keeping the family's financial struggles hidden? Or had she simply turned a blind eye to the corruption, believing that William would find a way to fix it all?

A Meeting with the Family Lawyer

Marlowe knew he needed more information. Henry Lawson, the family lawyer, had already shared crucial documents, including Charlotte's original will. But now, Marlowe needed to confront him about the family's financial situation.

Later that day, Marlowe met Lawson in his downtown office, the atmosphere heavy with tension. Lawson, always composed, looked more weary than usual, as if the weight of the Winthrop family's secrets had finally taken its toll on him.

"Detective," Lawson greeted him, motioning for Marlowe to take a seat. "I assume you've uncovered more than just family squabbles at this point."

Marlowe didn't waste time with pleasantries. "The Winthrop family is on the brink of financial collapse. William's been hiding it, moving money into offshore accounts. David's been embezzling funds to cover his gambling debts. And Charlotte—she found out. That's why she rewrote her will, isn't it? To protect her fortune from being swallowed up by the family's financial disaster."

Lawson nodded slowly, his expression grim. "You're correct. The family's wealth has been nothing more than a facade for some time now. William's been juggling debts, using every trick in the book to keep the family afloat, but it's only a matter of time before it all comes crashing down."

"And Charlotte knew?" Marlowe pressed.

"Yes," Lawson confirmed. "She discovered the truth when she began managing her own financial portfolio. She was furious—not just with William, but with David as well. She felt betrayed by both of them. That's when she came to me to rewrite her will. She wanted to distance herself from the family, both financially and emotionally."

Marlowe leaned forward, his voice low. "Did William know about the new will?"

Lawson hesitated for a moment before answering. "No. At least, not until after her death. He suspected something was wrong when Charlotte became more distant, but I don't believe he knew the full extent of her plans. If he had, I imagine he would have done everything in his power to stop her."

Marlowe's mind churned with possibilities. William's desperation to keep the family from falling apart, David's fear of exposure, and Charlotte's growing determination to free herself from the toxic legacy—it all led back to the same question: Who had the most to gain by silencing Charlotte?

Confrontation at the Estate

Later that evening, Marlowe returned to the Winthrop estate, the rain still pouring down in sheets. The once-pristine mansion now seemed like a hollow shell, a crumbling symbol of a family that had built its legacy on lies and deception.

He gathered the family in the drawing room—William, Eleanor, and David. The atmosphere was tense, each of them sensing that Marlowe had come to deliver a final blow.

"I've uncovered the truth about the family's finances," Marlowe began, his voice steady but firm. "The fortune you've all depended on isn't what it seems. William has been hiding the family's financial ruin, and David's been embezzling money to cover his gambling debts. And Charlotte—she found out. That's why she rewrote her will."

Eleanor gasped, her hand flying to her mouth. David shifted uncomfortably, his eyes darting to his father. William, however, remained stone-faced, though the tension in his jaw betrayed his anger.

"Charlotte was planning to leave," Marlowe continued, "and take her inheritance with her. If she had, it would have exposed everything. And without her money, the family would be left in ruins."

William's cold gaze finally met Marlowe's. "What are you accusing us of, Detective?"

"I'm saying that financial desperation drove someone to murder," Marlowe said, his voice rising. "Charlotte wasn't just a victim of a tragic accident. She was a threat to everything this family had built. And someone—whether it was you, William, or David—had a reason to stop her."

The room fell into a heavy silence, the weight of the accusation sinking in. Each of them had a motive. Each of them had something to lose.

But now, with the truth about the family's financial ruin laid bare, Marlowe knew that justice for Charlotte was finally within reach.

And as the rain continued to fall outside, he prepared to deliver the final blow that would bring the Winthrop dynasty crashing down.

Chapter 25: The Blackmail

The Winthrop estate felt like a house of cards on the verge of collapse. The rain continued its relentless assault outside, the rhythmic patter echoing the tension building inside. Detective Marlowe stood in the drawing room of the grand mansion, the dark truth of the family's financial ruin already laid bare. But there was another layer of deception that Marlowe was just beginning to uncover—one that threatened to expose not only new motives for Charlotte's death but also another suspect.

As Marlowe stared at the assembled family—William, Eleanor, and David—he knew that the final piece of the puzzle was still missing. And it had everything to do with blackmail.

A New Lead

It had been earlier that day when Marlowe received an anonymous tip. A message had been left at the station, a short, cryptic note:

The lake isn't the only thing drowning in secrets. Check her emails.

The message was typed, no signature, but it was enough to push Marlowe in a new direction. Immediately, he had requested access to Charlotte Winthrop's personal email and financial records. What he found was far more troubling than he could have anticipated.

Charlotte had been receiving anonymous messages for months—threatening emails, hinting at secrets from her past and leveraging her deepest fears. The emails alluded to something she had done, something someone was using against her.

But the most alarming part of it all was that Charlotte had been paying.

She had been sending large, untraceable payments through multiple accounts, payments meant to keep someone quiet. Whoever was behind the blackmail had been bleeding her dry financially, and it explained why she had grown more distant in the months leading up to her death. Charlotte had been caught in a web of fear, trying to keep her secret buried, all while planning her escape from the family.

As Marlowe read through the emails, the nature of the blackmail became clear. The sender had known about Charlotte's affair with Daniel Gresham, the man she had been in love with years ago—the man her father, William, had driven away. But it wasn't just the affair that was being used against her. The emails hinted at something darker—something that had happened at the lake during that time, a past incident that Charlotte had never spoken of.

The blackmailer had threatened to reveal everything if Charlotte didn't comply.

And she had been trapped, trying to buy her way out of the situation.

Confronting the Family

Marlowe faced the Winthrops, the weight of his new discovery pressing down on him. He knew that Charlotte had been targeted, but the question was: who had been behind the blackmail? The emails were anonymous, and the payments had been carefully routed to avoid detection. But Marlowe had one more card to play.

"Charlotte was being blackmailed," Marlowe said, his voice slicing through the tense silence of the room. "Someone knew about her past, about her affair with Daniel Gresham, and they were using it against her. She had been paying large sums of money to keep it quiet."

Eleanor's face paled, her hand trembling slightly as she clutched the armrest of her chair. "Blackmailed? By who?"

Marlowe fixed his gaze on William. "That's what I intend to find out. But I'm starting to think this wasn't just about her affair. The blackmailer knew something else—something that happened years ago at the lake."

William's jaw tightened, his eyes narrowing. "You're accusing one of us of blackmail? That's absurd."

Marlowe remained calm. "Is it? Charlotte had been trying to keep this secret buried, but the truth always has a way of coming out. And the person blackmailing her must have had access to very personal information. Information only someone close to her would know."

David, who had been staring at the floor, finally spoke, his voice hoarse. "You think one of us was blackmailing Charlotte?"

Marlowe didn't answer immediately. Instead, he reached into his coat pocket and pulled out a printed copy of one of the blackmail emails. He laid it on the coffee table between them, the words glaring up at the family.

You think you can run, but you can't hide from the past. You owe me, and if you don't want the world to know what really happened at the lake, you'll pay. Every last cent.

Eleanor let out a small gasp as she read the words, her hand covering her mouth in shock. William remained stoic, but his eyes betrayed the storm of emotions churning beneath the surface.

Marlowe stepped closer to David, his voice low but insistent. "You've been in financial trouble for a long time, David. You were desperate for money, and when you found out about Charlotte's affair—and the secret she was hiding—you saw an opportunity, didn't you?"

David's face flushed with anger. "I would never blackmail my own sister! I hated what was happening, yes, but I didn't... I couldn't have done that."

Marlowe studied him, reading the sincerity in his voice. He wasn't lying—not about this.

Then, he turned to William. "What about you, William? You've been manipulating your children for years, controlling every aspect of their lives. Could it have been you, blackmailing Charlotte to keep her from leaving? To keep her under your thumb?"

William stood abruptly, his fists clenched. "I protected this family! I did everything I could to maintain our legacy. But blackmail? No. That's beneath me."

Marlowe held William's gaze for a long moment. William might have controlled his children, but blackmail didn't fit his style. He was direct, forceful—he wouldn't have hidden behind anonymous emails.

But there was one person who had both the motive and the opportunity.

Marlowe turned slowly to Eleanor.

The room went deathly quiet as Marlowe's eyes locked on hers. Eleanor, who had always been in the background, the grieving mother, the quiet wife—she had known about Charlotte's affair, about the family's financial ruin. And she had been the one person no one had ever suspected.

Marlowe stepped closer, his voice soft but unwavering. "Eleanor. You knew everything, didn't you? You knew about Daniel Gresham, about the affair. You knew about the financial trouble William and David were in. And you knew about Charlotte's plan to leave, to take her fortune with her."

Eleanor's face drained of color, her eyes widening in fear. "I... I don't know what you're talking about..."

Marlowe didn't let up. "But you couldn't let her leave, could you? You couldn't let her walk away and abandon the family. So you blackmailed her—used her past against her to keep her in line."

Eleanor's breath hitched, and for a moment, Marlowe thought she might faint. But then, something shifted in her expression—a flicker of defiance.

"I did it for the family," Eleanor whispered, her voice trembling. "Charlotte was going to ruin everything. She was going to leave us with nothing. I couldn't let her destroy the Winthrop name. Not after everything we've built."

William stared at his wife in disbelief. "Eleanor, what have you done?"

Eleanor's eyes filled with tears, but her voice grew stronger. "I didn't want to hurt her. I thought if I pressured her, if I reminded her of what she stood to lose, she'd stay. But she wouldn't listen. She was determined to leave."

Marlowe stepped back, his heart heavy with the realization of what had truly happened. Eleanor's desperation to protect the family had led her down a dark path—one that had resulted in blackmail, manipulation, and ultimately, Charlotte's death.

"And when Charlotte refused to stay," Marlowe said quietly, "it all spiralled out of control, didn't it?"

Eleanor collapsed into a chair, sobbing. "I didn't mean for this to happen. I didn't mean to push her so far..."

Chapter 26: A Murderer Among Us

The air in the Winthrop estate felt thick, almost suffocating. The rain outside continued to batter the windows, a fitting backdrop for the storm brewing inside. Detective Marlowe stood in the center of the drawing room, facing the fractured family that had been torn apart by secrets, blackmail, and betrayal. He had uncovered the truth behind Charlotte's death, and now it was time to confront the family with the final revelation.

The faces of William, Eleanor, and David were tense, each reflecting a mixture of fear, anger, and anticipation. Marlowe had already exposed Eleanor's role in the blackmail scheme, but that was only part of the story. The real truth—the one that would finally tear apart the remnants of the Winthrop dynasty—was still to come.

Marlowe's voice broke the tense silence. "Charlotte's death wasn't an accident."

The words hung in the air like a bomb, and for a moment, no one moved. Then, almost as if on cue, the room erupted.

"What are you talking about?" William demanded, his voice sharp, his usual composure cracking. "David confessed. He said it was an accident!"

David, sitting in the corner, flinched at the mention of his name, guilt etched deeply into his face. "I didn't mean to kill her," he whispered, shaking his head. "I swear I didn't."

Marlowe turned to David, his eyes narrowing. "David, I believe you didn't mean to push her into the lake. But what happened that night wasn't just a tragic accident. It was the result of a series of choices—choices made by every member of this family."

Eleanor, still reeling from her earlier confession about the blackmail, looked at Marlowe with wide, tear-filled eyes. "What do you mean? I never wanted her to die. I only wanted to keep her from leaving..."

Marlowe took a deep breath, preparing for the final confrontation. "Charlotte was under immense pressure. She was being blackmailed by her own mother. She knew the family's financial ruin was imminent. And she was trying to break free from all of it—just like her mother, Margaret, and so many others before her. But someone in this room couldn't let that happen."

David looked up, confusion and fear clouding his expression. "You're saying someone else killed her?"

Marlowe nodded, his voice steady. "Yes. And I know who."

Reconstructing the Night of the Murder

Marlowe began to lay out the events of that fateful night, each detail adding weight to the revelation that was about to come.

"Charlotte had been planning to leave the family," Marlowe said. "She had rewritten her will, cutting David out and leaving her inheritance to charity. But more than that, she was preparing to expose the truth—about the family's finances, about the blackmail, about everything."

He glanced at William. "William, you were desperate to keep the family's financial collapse hidden. You had been moving money offshore, manipulating accounts to keep the illusion of wealth alive. You would have done anything to stop Charlotte from leaving and exposing your secrets."

William's eyes darkened, but he remained silent, his jaw clenched.

Marlowe continued, turning to David. "David, you were drowning in debt. Your gambling had spiralled out of control, and you had been embezzling money from the family business to cover your losses. When you found out that Charlotte was planning to leave and take her fortune with her, you panicked. You needed her money to survive."

David opened his mouth to protest, but Marlowe cut him off. "You followed her to the lake that night. You confronted her, desperate to make her stay. And in a moment of rage and fear, you pushed her."

David's face crumpled, tears spilling down his cheeks. "I didn't mean to," he sobbed. "I just wanted her to listen. I just wanted her to stay."

"But you didn't kill her," Marlowe said softly.

David looked up, confused. "What?"

Marlowe's gaze shifted to Eleanor, and the room seemed to freeze.

"Eleanor," Marlowe said, his voice low. "You knew what was happening. You had been blackmailing Charlotte, trying to keep her from leaving. But you also knew about David's financial troubles—and how much danger the family was in if Charlotte took her fortune with her."

Eleanor shook her head frantically. "No, no, I never wanted this. I didn't kill her—"

"You may not have pushed her into the lake," Marlowe interrupted, "but you knew what was happening. You were there that night, weren't you?"

Eleanor's face went white, her eyes wide with fear.

But the family's destruction had only just begun.

Leaving them with their thoughts, Marlow was suddenly called away.

Chapter 27: The Heiress's Last Words

Detective Marlowe stood in the dimly lit study, the glow from the small digital recorder in his hand casting faint shadows on the walls. It had been a long, gruelling investigation, filled with betrayals, blackmail, and a devastating loss of life. But now, with the discovery of Charlotte Winthrop's final message, the true depth of her despair—and her determination—was about to be revealed.

The recording had come to Marlowe unexpectedly. It had been found by one of the estate's staff in Charlotte's private sitting room, tucked away in a drawer beneath layers of old correspondence. The device was small, almost unassuming, but when Marlowe hit play, Charlotte's voice, filled with both vulnerability and strength, filled the room. It was her final act of defiance, her last attempt to make sense of the life she had tried so hard to escape.

Marlowe pressed play again, letting her words wash over him.

Charlotte's Voice, soft but steady:

If you're listening to this, then things have gotten worse than I ever imagined. I've tried to fight it, to break free of everything that's been holding me down, but it feels like there's no escape. Not from this family. Not from what they expect of me.

I've made mistakes. I've trusted the wrong people, believed the wrong things. And now I can feel it closing in on me. The secrets, the lies... They're like chains, and every time I try to break them, I'm pulled back in.

I know I've been distant, and I know my decisions have hurt some of the people I love. But I've been trying to protect myself. To protect what's left of me.

David, if you hear this... I'm sorry. I never wanted to hurt you. But I couldn't stay. I couldn't live in the shadow of this family any longer, pretending everything was fine when it wasn't. You deserved better than the life you've been trapped in. But so did I.

And Mother... (Charlotte's voice wavers here) I know you think you're doing what's right, that you're holding us all together. But you've lost sight of what matters. The lies you've told... they're eating us alive. You can't keep this family together with lies. It doesn't work. I can't live with it anymore.

A part of me wishes I could just disappear, that I could walk away from all of this and never look back. But I'm not sure anyone can ever really escape this family.

Marlowe paused the recording. Charlotte's words were raw, filled with the weight of her struggles. She had felt trapped—both by her family and by the expectations that had been placed on her since childhood. But what struck Marlowe most was her realization that her family's efforts to control and manipulate her were the very things that had pushed her to the edge.

The recording wasn't just a message; it was a cry for help, a plea to be understood, and an indictment of the people closest to her. But there was more.

Marlowe rewound the recording to the final part—Charlotte's voice taking on a tone of quiet dread as she spoke her last words.

Tonight, I'm going down to the lake. I don't know what will happen, but I can't hide from it anymore. I've been afraid for so long—afraid of the truth, of what they'll do if I leave. But I can't keep running. Not anymore.

If something happens to me... If you find this... Know that I didn't just give up. I tried to fight back. I tried to be free.

But freedom, I've learned, always comes at a price.

The recording clicked off, leaving Marlowe in silence. Charlotte's last words were a powerful admission of the fear that had driven her to the lake that night, the fear that had ultimately cost her her life.

Marlowe's mind raced. Charlotte hadn't been planning to leave quietly. She had gone to the lake knowing full well that something might happen to her. Whether it was David's confrontation or Eleanor's blackmail, Charlotte had been preparing for the worst.

But there was one final truth in her words: she hadn't given up. Charlotte had gone to the lake not to end things, but to fight for her freedom.

Revelation and Confrontation

With the recording in hand, Marlowe returned to the Winthrop estate's grand hall. William, Eleanor, and David were waiting for him, their expressions tight, wary. They had already been torn apart by the revelations of the previous days, but this—Charlotte's final words—would be the final blow.

Marlowe placed the recorder on the table in front of them, the silence in the room almost unbearable. "I found this in Charlotte's room. It's a recording she made the night she died."

Eleanor's hand flew to her mouth, and David's face drained of color. William remained motionless, but the tension in his posture was palpable.

Marlowe pressed play, and Charlotte's voice filled the room. Her words echoed off the walls, every sentence laden with emotion, each phrase cutting deeper than the last. As she spoke of her fear, her anger, her desire to be free, the weight of her suffering became impossible to ignore.

When the recording reached its end, the room remained silent. Eleanor was sobbing quietly, her body trembling with guilt. David's head was bowed, tears streaming down his face. And William... for the first time since Marlowe had met him, William Winthrop looked broken.

Marlowe broke the silence. "Charlotte wasn't just trying to run away. She was fighting for her life, for her freedom from this family. And she knew that something might happen to her."

David spoke first, his voice thick with emotion. "I didn't... I didn't know she felt like this. I thought she was leaving to punish us, to hurt us. But she just wanted to escape."

Eleanor, her voice barely a whisper, said, "I didn't want her to die... I just wanted her to stay. To hold the family together."

Marlowe's voice hardened. "But in trying to hold the family together, you destroyed her. Charlotte saw the lies, the manipulation, the control. And it killed her."

William, still silent, finally spoke. His voice was low, almost a whisper. "She was the only one who could have saved us."

Marlowe stared at him, his voice cold. "No, William. She was the only one who had the strength to break free. And you crushed her."

A Family in Ruins

As the truth of Charlotte's final moments settled over the room, it became clear that nothing would ever be the same for the Winthrop family. They had fought so hard to protect their name, their fortune, their legacy—but in the end, they had lost everything.

Charlotte's death had not just been a tragedy; it had been the inevitable result of a lifetime spent under the weight of expectations, control, and fear. And now, with her final words echoing in their minds, the family was left with nothing but their guilt.

Marlowe collected the recorder, turning to leave. His work here was done. Or so he thought!

As he stepped out into the cold, rainy night, he couldn't help but think of Charlotte's final words: Freedom always comes at a price.

For Charlotte, that price had been her life.

But for the Winthrop family, it had cost them everything.

And in the end, that was the true tragedy.

Chapter 28: The Boat House

Detective Marlowe stood at the edge of the Winthrop estate's lake, the waters dark and still under the brooding grey sky. The wind rustled through the tall pines, carrying with it the faint scent of rain and wet earth. The boat house, which had been abandoned since the night of Charlotte's death, loomed ahead, its old wooden walls weathered by years of neglect. Marlowe's gut told him that something crucial had been missed in the initial sweep of the area—something hidden, waiting to be found.

He had uncovered so much already: the financial ruin, the blackmail, the betrayals that had torn the Winthrop family apart. But despite all that, the final details of the night Charlotte died still felt incomplete. Her last words, preserved in the voice recording, had hinted at her fears, her determination to break free, and her understanding that something terrible might happen.

Now, Marlowe was certain the answer lay in the boat house. It was the one place that hadn't been fully explored, the one part of the estate where something might still be hidden.

The Boat House Revisited

Marlowe stepped through the creaking doorway of the boat house, his flashlight cutting through the gloom. Inside, the air was musty, thick with the smell of damp wood and stagnant water. Old oars and ropes hung from the rafters, and a small, overturned rowboat lay in the center of the floor. Dust and debris littered the ground, undisturbed since the night of Charlotte's death.

He had visited this place before, but it had seemed irrelevant at the time. There had been no signs of a struggle, no obvious evidence to suggest the boat house had played a role in what happened that night. But now, with everything he knew, Marlowe had a nagging suspicion that something had been overlooked.

His flashlight beam swept across the floor, illuminating the old wooden planks and cobweb-covered corners. He moved slowly, methodically, scanning every inch of the space.

Then something caught his eye.

In the far corner of the boat house, near the base of the wall, a loose floorboard was slightly raised. Marlowe crouched down, carefully prying it up with his gloved fingers. Beneath the board, nestled in the gap between the floorboards and the ground, was a small, metal object—dull, covered in dust, but unmistakable.

A key.

Marlowe's heart raced as he lifted the key from its hiding place. It was old, the kind that would unlock an antique chest or cabinet, but the question was: What had it been hidden here for? And what did it unlock?

As he examined the key, a thought occurred to him. There had been rumours in town, whispers about a secret that Charlotte had been keeping long before her death. And while Marlowe had already uncovered the blackmail and her plans to leave the family, he now wondered if there was something more—something Charlotte had hidden.

Something she had kept locked away.

The Hidden Chest

Marlowe returned to the mansion, his mind racing with possibilities. The key had to belong to something important—something Charlotte had hidden. As he walked through the grand halls of the Winthrop estate, his eyes scanned the rooms, searching for any sign of a locked cabinet or chest that might match the key's old-fashioned design.

He thought back to the nights he had spent combing through Charlotte's personal belongings, the journals, and letters. There had been an antique chest in her sitting room, a beautiful but inconspicuous piece of furniture that had seemed to hold nothing more than family heirlooms and old photographs. But perhaps there was more to it than met the eye.

Marlowe reached Charlotte's sitting room and approached the chest. It was made of dark wood, ornately carved, and slightly worn from years of use. He knelt in front of it and examined the lock. The keyhole was small, barely noticeable—but when he inserted the key he had found in the boat house, it fit perfectly.

With a soft click, the lock turned, and the chest opened.

Inside, beneath a layer of silk cloth, was a small bundle of letters tied together with a faded ribbon. Marlowe's pulse quickened as he carefully lifted the bundle out and untied the ribbon. These letters were different from the others he had found—they were addressed to Charlotte but signed with only a single initial: "D."

Marlowe's breath caught as he realized what he was holding. These were letters from Daniel Gresham, the man Charlotte had once loved and the man her father had driven away years ago.

A Secret Love Revealed

Marlowe sat down and began reading the letters. They were filled with passion, longing, and the pain of separation. Daniel had written to Charlotte during their secret affair, confessing his love for her and his desire to run away together. But there was more.

One letter, dated just weeks before Charlotte's death, stood out:

My Dearest Charlotte,

I can't believe we're here again, after all these years. It feels like fate, doesn't it? Like we were meant to find each other again after everything we've been through. But I can't help feeling the weight of the past bearing down on us.

I know you're afraid of what your family will do if they find out about us, but we can't keep living in the shadows. Your father tried to tear us apart once, but he can't control us anymore. You deserve to be free of them, free of the secrets and the lies.

Meet me at the lake tomorrow night. We'll talk about everything—about the future, about how we can finally be together. No more running.

Yours, always,

D.

Marlowe's mind raced. Daniel had been back in Charlotte's life, and they had been planning to meet at the lake on the night of her death. This wasn't just a story of blackmail and betrayal—it was a story of love, of a second chance that had been stolen from Charlotte.

But what had happened that night? Had Daniel been there when Charlotte died? Had their reunion been interrupted by the confrontation with David? And if so, why had Daniel disappeared without a trace?

Marlowe tucked the letters into his coat pocket. The key to solving Charlotte's death had been hidden all along—both in the boat house and in her heart. Daniel had been a part of her life, even at the end, and now, Marlowe needed to find him.

A New Suspect Emerges

As Marlowe left the mansion and headed back to town, the pieces of the puzzle began to fall into place. Charlotte had been trying to escape the control of her family, but she had also been trying to reunite with Daniel—a man she had loved but who had been forced out of her life. The night of her death, she had gone to the lake not just to confront her brother, but to meet Daniel and plan her escape.

But something had gone terribly wrong.

Marlowe now had to track down Daniel Gresham. The letters proved that he had been in contact with Charlotte shortly before her death, and his presence at the lake that night could change everything. If he had witnessed the confrontation, or worse, if he had been involved, then the story wasn't over yet.

The truth about Charlotte's death was within reach.

And with the discovery of the letters, a new suspect had emerged from the shadows.

Marlowe knew he had to act fast—before the real murderer slipped away for good.

Chapter 29: A Sister's Lies

The discovery of the letters in the antique chest had shifted the investigation, placing Daniel Gresham at the center of Charlotte's final days. But just as Detective Marlowe began piecing together the love story that had haunted Charlotte, a knock on his office door brought everything to a grinding halt.

The woman who stepped through the door was not someone Marlowe recognized. She carried herself with a calm, almost eerie confidence, her sharp eyes taking in every detail of the room before settling on Marlowe.

"Detective Marlowe?" she asked, her voice measured but laced with tension.

"That's right," Marlowe said, standing to greet her. "And you are?"

She hesitated, as if calculating her words carefully. "My name is Lydia Winthrop."

Marlowe's brow furrowed. Another Winthrop? This woman had not been mentioned in any of the family histories he had reviewed, nor had any of the surviving family members referenced her.

"And how exactly are you related to the Winthrop family?" he asked, his curiosity piqued.

Lydia's lips tightened. "I'm Charlotte's half-sister. And I've been keeping a secret for far too long."

The Hidden Truth

Marlowe leaned forward, his mind racing. Another Winthrop sibling, hidden from the public and the rest of the family? The revelation felt almost surreal. "Go on," he said, trying to maintain his composure. "What kind of secret?"

Lydia took a deep breath, then slowly pulled an envelope from her purse and slid it across Marlowe's desk. "It's all in here," she said. "This is the evidence you need."

Marlowe opened the envelope carefully, his eyes scanning the contents. Inside were legal documents, correspondence, and a birth certificate. The certificate named William Winthrop as Lydia's father, but the mother's name was one Marlowe didn't recognize: Emily Dawes.

Marlowe's gaze flicked up to Lydia. "Your mother...?"

"She was William's mistress," Lydia said bluntly. "He had an affair with her before he married Eleanor. I was the result. But William never acknowledged me publicly. He paid for my education, kept my mother comfortable, but I was always kept in the shadows."

The detective's mind spun as he absorbed the implications of this revelation. William Winthrop, always so concerned with the public image of his family, had hidden an illegitimate child. And while that might have been scandalous enough on its own, Lydia's presence raised even more questions.

"Why are you coming forward now?" Marlowe asked, his tone cautious.

Lydia's eyes flashed with a mixture of anger and sadness. "I didn't want to be involved. I stayed away, as he asked. But after Charlotte's death, I couldn't keep quiet anymore. I have information about what really happened to her."

Marlowe's heart skipped a beat. "What do you mean?"

"Charlotte and I... we knew about each other," Lydia explained. "She found out the truth years ago. At first, she was furious, felt betrayed. But eventually, she reached out to me. We started writing letters, meeting in secret. We became close."

Marlowe leaned in, his instincts kicking into high gear. "And what did you talk about?"

"Everything," Lydia said. "Our father, our family... Charlotte confided in me about the pressures she was under. She told me about Daniel Gresham, about how she wanted to leave the family and start a new life. But most importantly, she told me about the inheritance."

Marlowe's eyes narrowed. "The inheritance?"

Lydia nodded. "William had promised Charlotte the full estate, but only if she continued to stay and run the family business. When Charlotte told him she was planning to leave, he changed his mind. He was going to cut her out of the will entirely and leave everything to David instead."

Marlowe leaned back in his chair, his mind racing. William had threatened to cut Charlotte off financially, knowing that it would leave her with nothing. That, combined with the blackmail and her secret relationship with Daniel, must have pushed her to the brink.

"But there's more," Lydia continued, her voice growing quieter. "The night Charlotte died, she sent me a message. She told me that something was wrong, that she was afraid."

Marlowe stiffened. "What kind of message?"

Lydia pulled out her phone and scrolled through her messages before handing it to Marlowe. The screen displayed a short but chilling text from Charlotte, sent just hours before her death:

"He knows. I'm going to the lake tonight. I don't know what's going to happen, but if something goes wrong, please don't let them cover it up. They can't keep doing this."

Marlowe felt a chill run down his spine. Charlotte had known. She had been aware that someone—perhaps her father or David—was planning something. She had gone to the lake that night expecting a confrontation.

"What did she mean by 'he knows'?" Marlowe asked, looking up from the phone.

Lydia shook her head. "I don't know for sure. But I think she was talking about our father. She must have found out that he was planning to disinherit her—and that he knew about her plans with Daniel."

Marlowe sat back, trying to piece it all together. Charlotte had been trapped on all sides—by her father's manipulations, by the financial ruin looming over the family, by her brother's resentment. And now,

Lydia's presence added another layer of complexity. Had William known about her? Had Charlotte's discovery of her half-sister's existence been the final straw that shattered the fragile balance within the family?

The Confrontation

Later that day, Marlowe returned to the Winthrop estate, this time with Lydia by his side. The time for secrets was over, and it was time to confront the family with the truth.

William, Eleanor, and David were gathered in the sitting room once again when Marlowe entered, their expressions shifting from surprise to unease as they saw Lydia with him.

"What is this?" William demanded, his voice cold and sharp.

"This," Marlowe said, "is Lydia Winthrop. Your daughter."

The room fell deathly silent. Eleanor gasped, her hand flying to her mouth. David's face went pale, his eyes darting between Lydia and his father. William, however, stood perfectly still, his face unreadable.

"Lydia is your daughter with Emily Dawes," Marlowe continued, his voice steady. "Charlotte knew about her, and they were in contact for years. She confided in Lydia about the pressures she was under, about her plan to leave the family. And most importantly, Charlotte told Lydia that she was afraid—afraid of what would happen the night she died."

William's expression darkened, but he said nothing.

"Charlotte sent Lydia a message just hours before her death," Marlowe pressed on, holding up the phone with the message displayed. "She said she was going to the lake, that she thought something was going to happen. And she said, 'he knows.'"

Eleanor's eyes filled with tears as she looked at her husband. "William, what have you done?"

William's voice was low and menacing. "I did what I had to do to protect this family. Charlotte was going to ruin everything. She was going to leave, take everything with her. I couldn't let her destroy us."

David, who had been silent until now, suddenly stood. "You knew? You knew she was going to the lake that night?"

William turned to him, his face twisted with anger. "Of course I knew. She was going to meet that man, Daniel Gresham. She was going to leave us all behind."

David's voice trembled with rage. "You... you let this happen? You let her die?"

Marlowe stepped forward, his voice sharp. "William, did you plan to kill Charlotte?"

William's eyes flickered with something—fear, perhaps—but he didn't answer. His silence was all the confirmation Marlowe needed.

Charlotte had been caught in a web of lies and manipulation, her fate sealed by the very people who were supposed to protect her. And now, with the truth of Lydia's existence and the damning message she had received, the full picture had finally come into focus.

The Final Collapse

As Marlowe left the estate, the weight of the Winthrop family's secrets pressed down on him. Lydia's revelation had shattered whatever remained of the family's fragile unity. William's lies, Eleanor's guilt, and David's grief were now laid bare for the world to see.

But Charlotte's story—her tragic fight for freedom—had finally been told. And in the end, it was her half-sister, the one she had secretly embraced, who had delivered the final blow.

The Winthrop dynasty had crumbled, brought down by the very lies it had tried so hard to conceal.

And the truth, as always, had set the final pieces in motion.

Chapter 30: The Missing Witness

Detective Marlowe stared at the lead that had just come across his desk, his heart quickening with the sudden realization that the final piece of the puzzle might be within his grasp. The investigation into Charlotte Winthrop's death had taken many unexpected turns—blackmail, financial ruin, a hidden sister, and a web of lies that had trapped everyone involved. But one nagging detail had remained elusive: a missing witness.

Since the beginning of the investigation, there had been rumours of someone who had seen something that night at the lake. It was a small, almost forgotten mention from a local, someone claiming that a stranger had been spotted near the estate, watching from a distance. That rumour had resurfaced in whispers around town, and now, Marlowe had finally tracked down the person who could bring the case to its conclusion.

The witness was a man named Samuel Tate, a local fisherman who had been living off the grid for years. He often kept to himself, spending his days on the lake in his small boat, fishing and staying out of trouble. It wasn't until someone recognized his description from that night that Marlowe had a chance to find him.

The word had come through an informant: Samuel Tate had been near the Winthrop estate the night Charlotte died. He had seen something, but for reasons of his own, he had stayed silent. Until now.

The Fisherman's Story

Marlowe arrived at a small cabin on the outskirts of town, nestled deep in the woods by the water's edge. The air was thick with the smell of pine and wet earth as he knocked on the door, hearing the sound of footsteps inside.

Samuel Tate opened the door, his face weathered by years of exposure to the elements. His eyes were sharp, though, and as he looked Marlowe over, there was a flicker of recognition.

"You're the detective investigating that Winthrop girl's death," Samuel said, his voice gruff but steady.

"That's right," Marlowe replied. "And I think you know something about what happened that night."

Samuel hesitated for a moment, then stepped aside, letting Marlowe enter the cabin. The interior was sparse—just a table, a few chairs, and fishing gear stacked in the corner. Samuel gestured for Marlowe to sit as he poured two cups of coffee, his movements deliberate and slow.

For a moment, neither man spoke. Then, Samuel finally broke the silence. "I wasn't looking to get involved in their mess, you know. Rich folks, their problems—they ain't got nothing to do with me. But that night..." He paused, his eyes distant. "I saw something I couldn't ignore."

Marlowe leaned forward, his heart pounding. "Tell me what you saw."

Samuel took a sip of his coffee, his hand shaking slightly. "I was out on the lake that night. The storm was rolling in, and I figured I'd catch a few more fish before heading back to shore. But as I got closer to the Winthrop estate, I saw someone by the lake. At first, I didn't think much of it—people come out there sometimes, just to walk. But then I saw another person, moving in the shadows, like they were watching from the trees."

Marlowe's pulse quickened. "Do you know who it was?"

Samuel shook his head. "Not at first. But I heard them arguing—one of the voices was a woman's. She sounded scared, desperate. The other voice... it was low, angry. I couldn't make out all the words, but it wasn't good. I stayed back, didn't want to be seen, but then I saw the man step out from the trees."

Marlowe's grip on his coffee mug tightened. "Who was the man?"

Samuel's eyes flickered with something close to regret. "It was her brother. David Winthrop."

THE DROWNED HEIRESS 143

Marlowe's breath caught in his throat. He had suspected David from the beginning, but the situation had been complicated by Eleanor's blackmail, William's manipulation, and Charlotte's complicated relationship with Daniel. Now, with this witness confirming David's presence at the lake, the pieces were finally falling into place.

"What happened next?" Marlowe asked, his voice barely above a whisper.

"They were shouting at each other," Samuel continued. "I couldn't hear everything, but I heard David say something about the will. About how she was going to ruin everything. I saw him grab her, shake her. And then..." Samuel's voice trailed off as he stared down into his cup. "He pushed her."

Marlowe's heart sank. "Into the lake?"

Samuel nodded, his face pale. "She fell into the water, and I thought for sure she'd come back up, but she didn't. I saw David standing there, staring at the water, like he couldn't believe what he'd done. And then he just... ran."

The silence that followed was heavy, filled with the weight of Samuel's words. David had pushed Charlotte into the lake. He had killed her, whether by accident or in a fit of rage, it didn't matter anymore.

Samuel cleared his throat, looking up at Marlowe with a pained expression. "I should've said something sooner. But I didn't want to get involved. People like me—we don't meddle in the lives of people like the Winthrops. I'm sorry."

Marlowe stood, his mind racing. Samuel's confession was the final piece of the puzzle, the one that would finally allow him to close the case and confront the killer.

Chapter 31: The Confrontation

Detective Marlowe stood in the grand foyer of the Winthrop estate, his heart pounding as he prepared for the final, inevitable confrontation. The truth about Charlotte's death had been pieced together bit by bit—financial ruin, blackmail, a hidden half-sister, and now, the missing witness who had seen the fatal moment. But there was one last thread to unravel: the true killer.

Though David had confessed to pushing Charlotte into the lake, something about his confession still felt incomplete. Marlowe had sensed that David's guilt and despair had clouded his memory of that night, but now, after reviewing all the evidence and testimonies, the final puzzle pieces had clicked into place.

And the truth was even more twisted than he had expected.

As Marlowe walked through the silent hallways, his footsteps echoing on the marble floor, the weight of everything he had uncovered pressed heavily on him. Tonight, he would confront the person responsible for orchestrating Charlotte's death, and he knew the family would never be the same.

The drawing room came into view, its massive fireplace casting flickering shadows across the walls. Inside, William, Eleanor, David, and Lydia were gathered, their faces pale and strained. They had been summoned by Marlowe, each of them bracing for the final blow. The air was thick with tension, the unspoken accusations hanging between them like a shroud.

Marlowe stepped inside, his eyes sweeping over the room before settling on William Winthrop, the family patriarch. The man who had controlled and manipulated everyone around him for years.

"I've gathered you all here tonight to put an end to this," Marlowe began, his voice steady but hard. "We've all been searching for answers, for the truth behind Charlotte's death. And now, after weeks of investigation, I have the final piece of the puzzle."

The room was deathly silent. Eleanor clutched the arm of her chair, her knuckles white, while David sat rigidly, his face a mixture of guilt and fear. Lydia, the once-hidden sister, watched from the corner, her expression unreadable. But it was William who held Marlowe's gaze, his eyes narrowing in suspicion.

"You've all tried to cover up your roles in this," Marlowe continued, "but in the end, only one person truly orchestrated the events that led to Charlotte's death. One person who manipulated everyone else, driven by greed, control, and fear of losing everything."

William's jaw clenched. "We've all suffered enough, Detective. What are you implying?"

Marlowe stepped forward, his voice sharp. "I'm not implying anything, William. I'm saying that Charlotte's death wasn't just an accident or an act of desperation by David. It was something much darker—something you orchestrated."

The room erupted.

"What?" David shot to his feet, his face contorted in confusion. "I pushed her! I killed her!"

"No," Marlowe said calmly, turning to face David. "You pushed her, yes. But you didn't kill her."

David's face twisted in disbelief. "But I saw her fall into the lake. I saw her—"

Marlowe shook his head. "She didn't die from the fall into the lake, David. When you pushed her, she hit the water, but she was still alive."

David collapsed back into his chair, his hands shaking. "What do you mean?"

Marlowe's gaze hardened as he looked directly at William. "Charlotte would have survived that night. She would have come up from the water, but someone else was there. Someone who wanted to make sure she didn't."

William's face remained cold, impassive, though a flicker of something passed through his eyes—fear, perhaps, or realization.

"Charlotte was planning to leave the family, to take her inheritance and walk away from everything," Marlowe said, his voice rising. "You couldn't allow that, William. Not with the family on the verge of financial collapse, not with all the secrets you've been hiding. So you did what you've always done—you took control."

Eleanor gasped, her hand flying to her mouth. "William... no..."

Marlowe continued relentlessly. "You knew Charlotte was going to the lake that night. You knew she was meeting with Daniel Gresham. And you knew she had finally made up her mind to leave. That's why you followed her to the lake, didn't you?"

William's expression darkened, but he said nothing.

Marlowe stepped closer, his voice filled with accusation. "You were there, hiding in the shadows, watching everything. You saw David push her. And when Charlotte hit the water, you had a choice—you could save her, or you could let her drown."

David's eyes widened in horror. "No... no, that can't be true."

Marlowe turned to him, his voice softer. "You weren't the one who killed her, David. William waited until you ran. He stood there, watching her struggle in the water. And then he did nothing. He let her drown."

The silence that followed was suffocating, broken only by Eleanor's quiet sobs and David's ragged breathing. Lydia sat perfectly still, her eyes locked on William.

"William," Marlowe said, his voice cutting through the tension like a blade, "you wanted to control everything, even your children. You couldn't let Charlotte leave because it would have exposed everything—the financial ruin, the blackmail, the lies. So you let her die."

William's face, usually a mask of control, cracked. His eyes flashed with fury as he finally spoke. "She was going to destroy everything I built! She didn't understand what was at stake. She was reckless, ungrateful. I did what I had to do to protect this family."

David stood up, shaking with anger and disbelief. "You let her die? You stood there and did nothing?"

William's gaze flicked to his son, but there was no remorse in his expression. "She would have left us all to ruin. I couldn't let that happen."

Eleanor's sobs grew louder, her body trembling as the full horror of what had happened sank in. Lydia, who had remained silent, finally stood, her voice cold and unfeeling. "You killed her."

William turned to Lydia, his face twisted with rage. "You don't understand—"

"I understand perfectly," Lydia interrupted, her voice steady. "You never cared about her, or any of us. It was always about control."

Marlowe watched the confrontation unfold, his heart heavy with the weight of the truth. William Winthrop, the powerful patriarch, had been willing to sacrifice his own daughter to protect his legacy. His greed, his need for control, had ultimately led to Charlotte's tragic death.

The family, once united under the illusion of power and wealth, was now shattered beyond repair.

The Unmasking

As the confrontation reached its climax, Marlowe stepped forward, his voice resolute. "William Winthrop, you're under arrest for the murder of Charlotte Winthrop."

William's face remained defiant, but there was no denying the truth anymore. The room seemed to shrink around him as the weight of his actions closed in, the walls of the grand estate—once a symbol of his power—now a prison of his own making.

David, still in shock, turned away, unable to look at his father. Eleanor wept quietly, her world crumbling before her eyes, while Lydia stood firm, the sister who had remained hidden finally watching justice unfold.

As Marlowe placed the handcuffs on William, the full tragedy of the Winthrop family's fall became clear. They had been destroyed not by external forces, but by the very thing they had fought so hard to protect—their own legacy.

Charlotte had tried to break free, but her father's obsession with control had cost her her life.

And in the end, William Winthrop had been unmasked as the true killer.

As Marlowe led him out of the room, the cold night air met them at the door. The storm that had been brewing around the Winthrop family for years had finally broken.

And now, all that remained was the aftermath.

Justice had been served, but the price was more than any of them could have ever imagined.

Chapter 32: The Heiress's Revenge

The Winthrop estate loomed dark and silent against the evening sky, its once-grand halls now haunted by the truth of what had transpired. Detective Marlowe stood on the front steps, the cold wind biting at his skin as he watched the police car disappear down the long driveway, carrying William Winthrop—the man who had allowed his own daughter to drown.

Charlotte Winthrop's death had been the result of greed, control, and betrayal, all orchestrated by the patriarch who had shaped and manipulated everyone in his family. But now, the truth was out. The man who had spent his life building a legacy of power and wealth would spend the rest of his days behind bars, his empire in ruins.

But for Marlowe, the sense of justice remained elusive.

He turned his gaze back to the mansion. The Winthrop family had been destroyed, not just by William's crime, but by years of secrets and lies that had finally come to light. Charlotte had fought for her freedom, and though she hadn't lived to see it, her fight had brought the family to its knees. Now, it was time to ensure her story didn't end in silence.

The Legal Reckoning

The courtroom was packed with reporters, the media eager to cover the scandal that had rocked one of the city's most powerful families. William Winthrop sat in the defendant's chair, his face gaunt and pale. He was no longer the imposing figure who had commanded respect and fear; he was a broken man, haunted by the consequences of his actions.

Marlowe had worked tirelessly with the prosecution to build a case that would leave no room for doubt. The key witnesses—David, Eleanor, and even Lydia—had all provided damning testimony, detailing the depths of William's manipulation and control. But it was the discovery of Samuel Tate, the fisherman who had witnessed the events by the lake, that had sealed William's fate. His testimony had been the final piece, proving that William had watched his daughter die and done nothing to save her.

As the judge delivered the verdict—guilty of second-degree murder—a murmur ran through the courtroom. William remained silent, his eyes fixed on the floor. The once-great patriarch was now nothing more than a criminal, his carefully constructed legacy in tatters.

For Charlotte, justice had been served through the legal system. William would spend the rest of his life in prison, stripped of the power he had wielded over his family for so long. His wealth, his status, everything he had fought to protect, had been torn away.

But even as the gavel came down and the courtroom emptied, Marlowe couldn't shake the feeling that the true cost of this justice had been far too high.

A More Personal Justice

That evening, after the trial had concluded, Marlowe returned to the lake, where it had all begun. The water lay still under the dark sky, reflecting the stars above. It was peaceful now, but Marlowe could feel the weight of the past lingering here—the place where Charlotte had been taken from the world.

He stood on the shore, his thoughts heavy. Justice, in its legal form, had been served. But something inside him still churned. William's imprisonment couldn't erase the pain and destruction he had caused. Charlotte's death still felt unresolved, like an open wound that had been bandaged but never truly healed.

As he stared out at the water, a figure appeared beside him. It was Lydia, her presence almost ghostly in the quiet night.

"I thought I'd find you here," she said softly, her eyes reflecting the same sorrow that Marlowe felt.

Marlowe didn't respond immediately. He simply nodded, letting the silence between them settle.

"Do you think this is enough?" Lydia asked after a while. "Will what happened to Charlotte ever feel... right?"

Marlowe shook his head. "I don't think so. The law can punish William for what he did, but it can't bring her back. It can't undo the years of damage he caused."

Lydia sighed, folding her arms as she stared out at the lake. "She deserved better. She fought so hard to break free, but in the end, it was her fight that killed her."

Marlowe's jaw clenched. "She did what she could, and in the end, her fight brought down everything William built. That's something."

Lydia turned to him, her expression unreadable. "But it's not enough, is it?"

Marlowe met her gaze, the unspoken tension hanging in the air. He knew what Lydia was suggesting—something more than just legal justice. Something personal. The Winthrops had ruined lives, not just within their family but beyond. There was still a darkness in William, a sense that even from behind bars, he would find a way to hold onto some piece of his power.

Lydia stepped closer, her voice low. "I know you want justice for Charlotte. Real justice. The kind that makes sure men like William never hurt anyone again."

Marlowe looked at her, his mind racing. He had always believed in the law, in due process. But after everything he had seen, after all the pain that had been caused, something inside him stirred. An idea—dark, but undeniable—crept into his thoughts. Was there another kind of justice?

Lydia's eyes flashed with determination. "I know people. People who can make sure William never has the chance to hurt anyone else. People who can make sure his prison sentence is more than just a cage. It can be a reckoning."

Marlowe hesitated, the weight of the decision pressing down on him. This wasn't just about the law anymore. This was about vengeance, about ensuring that the man who had destroyed so many lives would feel the full force of the pain he had caused.

He turned back to the lake, his thoughts swirling.

"Charlotte deserves peace," Lydia whispered. "And so do you."

The Heiress's Revenge

In the weeks that followed, William Winthrop began his prison sentence. But something shifted behind the scenes.

Charlotte's revenge had been delivered, not just by the law, but by those who ensured her father would never have another moment of peace.

As Marlowe stood once more by the lake, months after the trial, he felt a strange sense of calm. The heiress had been avenged, in every way possible. The legacy of the Winthrop family was no more, and the man who had caused so much pain was now nothing but a shadow of his former self.

Justice had been served.

But whether it was the kind that Charlotte would have wanted, Marlowe would never truly know.

The water lapped gently at the shore, the stars reflected in the calm surface. For the first time since Charlotte's death, the estate felt quiet—truly at peace.

And that, Marlowe thought, was what mattered most.

Chapter 33: The Detective's Reflection

Detective Marlowe sat in the small corner café, the sounds of the city bustling around him, yet somehow feeling distant. The case of Charlotte Winthrop had finally come to an end, but the lingering effects of everything he had uncovered remained heavy on his mind. The steam from his coffee curled into the air, but Marlowe wasn't focused on the present—he was lost in the past, in the lessons learned from the downfall of one of the wealthiest and most powerful families in the city.

The Winthrop case had been unlike any other he had ever worked on. It wasn't just about the death of an heiress—it was a story of greed, power, control, and the slow unravelling of a family that had built its empire on lies. Marlowe had walked into the investigation expecting to find a simple explanation for Charlotte's tragic death, but what he had discovered was far more complex. It had forced him to confront the darker truths about wealth, legacy, and the lengths people would go to preserve the illusion of control.

The Illusion of Power

Marlowe had seen the destructive force of power up close. William Winthrop had built his life around controlling everyone and everything in his orbit, believing that wealth and influence gave him the right to dictate the lives of those around him. His control had extended not just to his business empire but to his family, manipulating them to serve his needs, even at the cost of their happiness and freedom.

And it was that very control that had led to Charlotte's death.

Sipping his coffee, Marlowe reflected on the illusion of power that had consumed William. He had believed that by controlling his children, his finances, and his legacy, he could secure his place in the world, untouchable by the consequences of his actions. But in the end, his desire for control had been his undoing. It had destroyed his family, shattered his carefully constructed life, and left him a broken man.

Power, Marlowe realized, was a fleeting thing. It could protect people for a time, but once cracks began to form, everything could come crashing down. William's wealth hadn't saved him from the consequences of his actions. It had only delayed the inevitable collapse.

The detective wondered how many other families, propped up by wealth and influence, were just as fragile as the Winthrops had been—how many were one secret, one betrayal away from falling apart.

Wealth and Legacy

As Marlowe stared out the café window, watching people go about their daily lives, he thought about the concept of legacy. The Winthrops had been obsessed with theirs. William had sacrificed everything to maintain the family's name and status, while Charlotte had fought to escape the suffocating expectations that came with her inheritance.

But in the end, what did legacy mean? Was it simply the wealth one left behind? The power one wielded? Or was it the impact one had on the people around them?

Charlotte had tried to leave a different kind of legacy—one built not on wealth, but on freedom. She had rewritten her will, cutting her family out and leaving her fortune to charity, in the hope of creating something better for herself and others. But even that decision had been tainted by the very forces she sought to escape. Her fight to be free had cost her everything.

Marlowe wondered if it had been worth it. Charlotte had been brave, but the chains of the Winthrop name had been too heavy, even for her. In the end, she had been consumed by the very thing she had tried to leave behind.

Wealth, Marlowe thought, was a double-edged sword. It could offer comfort and opportunity, but it also brought with it expectations, responsibilities, and a certain kind of moral compromise. The

Winthrops had been trapped by their wealth, forced to maintain an image that no longer aligned with who they were.

For Marlowe, the case had been a stark reminder that wealth was not synonymous with happiness or peace. The Winthrop estate had been a prison, not just for Charlotte, but for the entire family.

Moral Ambiguity

But perhaps the most troubling part of the case for Marlowe had been the moral ambiguity. He had always believed in justice, in the black-and-white nature of right and wrong. But the Winthrop case had forced him to confront the shades of grey.

William Winthrop had been the villain in many ways—he had let his daughter die, and his manipulation had set the events in motion. Yet, in his mind, he had acted out of necessity, out of a desire to protect what he had built. Eleanor, too, had believed she was doing the right thing by blackmailing Charlotte, thinking that her lies were holding the family together. Even David, who had pushed his sister, had acted out of desperation, blinded by his own insecurities and fear of being left behind.

None of them were innocent, yet none were purely evil either. They were flawed, trapped in a web of their own making.

And then there was Marlowe himself.

He had allowed Lydia's suggestion of a more personal justice for William to play out, knowing that the legal system could never fully deliver the retribution that Charlotte deserved. He had let it happen, knowing that it was a step into the moral grey area he had always tried to avoid. And now, he couldn't shake the feeling that he had become complicit in something darker.

Had it been the right thing to do? Charlotte had found her revenge, but Marlowe couldn't help but feel a sense of unease. He had crossed a line, one that he might never be able to uncross.

Justice, he realized, wasn't always clean. Sometimes it required choices that weighed heavily on the soul. And in the Winthrop case, justice had been served—but at what cost?

Lessons Learned

As Marlowe finished his coffee and prepared to leave, he knew that the Winthrop case would stay with him for a long time. It had forced him to confront uncomfortable truths about wealth, power, and the fragile nature of legacy. It had shown him that those with the most often had the most to lose—and that the price of maintaining control could be devastating.

Charlotte's fight for freedom had been noble, but in the end, she had been a victim of forces larger than herself. Her family, consumed by their own ambition and fear, had destroyed everything they had once claimed to protect.

But perhaps the most important lesson Marlowe had learned was about himself. The moral compromises he had made, the choices that had blurred the line between justice and vengeance—these were things he would carry with him, even after the case was closed.

As he stepped out of the café and into the cold night air, Marlowe knew that he would continue to pursue the truth, no matter how dark or ambiguous it became. But he also knew that the Winthrop case had changed him.

The world, he realized, was far more complicated than he had once believed.

And justice? It was never as simple as it seemed.

Disclaimer

This is a work of fiction. Names, characters, places, and incidents are either the product of the author's imagination or used fictitiously. Any resemblance to actual persons, living or dead, events, or locales is entirely coincidental.

The author has made every effort to ensure the accuracy of historical, legal, and procedural details in the context of the story, but certain liberties have been taken for dramatic purposes. This book is not intended to provide an accurate representation of any real legal proceedings, investigations, or events.

The views and opinions expressed by the characters do not reflect those of the author, publisher, or any entity associated with this publication.

Milton Keynes UK
Ingram Content Group UK Ltd.
UKHW031144311024
450535UK00001B/19